W9-AET-622

A Cat
Under the
Mistletoe

The Intriguing Mysteries of Lydia Adamson

Other Books in the Alice Nestleton mystery series

A CAT IN THE MANGER
A CAT OF A DIFFERENT COLOR
A CAT IN WOLF'S CLOTHING
A CAT BY ANY OTHER NAME
A CAT IN THE WINGS
A CAT WITH A FIDDLE
A CAT IN A GLASS HOUSE
A CAT WITH NO REGRETS
A CAT ON THE CUTTING EDGE
A CAT ON A WINNING STREAK
A CAT IN FINE STYLE
A CAT IN A CHORUS LINE

The Deirdre Quinn Nightingale mysteries

DR. NIGHTINGALE COMES HOME
DR. NIGHTINGALE RIDES THE ELEPHANT
DR. NIGHTINGALE GOES TO THE DOGS
DR. NIGHTINGALE GOES THE DISTANCE
DR. NIGHTINGALE ENTERS THE BEAR CAVE
DR. NIGHTINGALE RIDES TO HOUNDS
DR. NIGHTINGALE CHASES THREE LITTLE PIGS

*. . . and the first book in the new Lucy Wales
mystery series*

BEWARE THE TUFTED DUCK

A Cat Under the the Mistletoe

AN ALICE NESTLETON MYSTERY

Lydia Adamson

NEW HANOVER COUNTY
PUBLIC LIBRARY
201 CHESTNUT STREET
WILMINGTON, N C 28401

A DUTTON BOOK

DUTTON
Published by the Penguin Group
Penguin Books USA Inc., 375 Hudson Street,
New York, New York 10014, U.S.A.
Penguin Books Ltd, 27 Wrights Lane, London W8 5TZ, England
Penguin Books Australia Ltd, Ringwood, Victoria, Australia
Penguin Books Canada Ltd, 10 Alcorn Avenue,
Toronto, Ontario, Canada M4V 3B2
Penguin Books (N.Z.) Ltd, 182–190 Wairau Road,
Auckland 10, New Zealand

Penguin Books Ltd, Registered Offices:
Harmondsworth, Middlesex, England

First published by Dutton, an imprint of Dutton Signet,
a division of Penguin Books USA Inc.
Distributed in Canada by McClelland & Stewart Inc.

First Printing, October, 1996
10 9 8 7 6 5 4 3 2 1

Copyright © Lydia Adamson, 1996
All rights reserved

REGISTERED TRADEMARK—MARCA REGISTRADA

LIBRARY OF CONGRESS CATALOGING-IN-PUBLICATION DATA:
Adamson, Lydia.
    A cat under the mistletoe : an Alice Nestleton mystery / Lydia
Adamson.
        p. cm.
    ISBN 0-525-94226-2
    1. Nestleton, Alice (Fictitious character)—Fiction.   2. Women
detectives—United States—Fiction.   3. Actresses—United States—
Fiction. 4. Cats—Fiction. I. Title.
PS3551.D3954C44 1996
813'.54—dc20   96-16145
                                                     CIP

Printed in the United States of America

PUBLISHER'S NOTE
This is a work of fiction. Names, characters, places, and incidents
either are the products of the author's imagination or are used ficti-
tiously, and any resemblance to actual persons, living or dead,
events, or locales is entirely coincidental.

Without limiting the rights under copyright reserved above, no part
of this publication may be reproduced, stored in or introduced into
a retrieval system, or transmitted, in any form, or by any means
(electronic, mechanical, photocopying, recording, or otherwise),
without the prior written permission of both the copyright owner
and the above publisher of this book.

This book is printed on acid-free paper. ∞

A Cat
Under the
Mistletoe

Chapter 1

I always seem to end up in strange places with strange cats.

It was six-thirty on a chilly late fall morning, a few weeks before Christmas. I was sitting in a taxi that was hurtling north on Eighth Avenue. Traffic was light and the cabby almost seemed to be flying up the avenue.

Next to me on the backseat was a carrier, and in the carrier was a cat named Roberta. She was a dainty shorthaired white cat with ears and eyes too big for her body and brown splotches on her rump, left shoulder, and left ear.

I had picked Roberta up at her very posh lower Fifth Avenue domicile and was bringing her to an animal psychologist on Central Park West to get her dear little head straightened out.

How I ended up in that cab with that cat is not really a mystery.

My friend Nora Karroll, who owns a bistro called Pal Joey in the theater district, became friendly with one of her longtime bistro denizens, Joseph Vise.

Vise is one of those "almost famous" character actors. Everybody knows him but nobody knows his name. He is getting on in age now, and he alternates between playing lovable grandfathers and ruthless old Mafia dons.

He had been offered a small part in a TV movie that was shooting out of town, and he needed a cat-sitter for his lovely little shorthaired tortoiseshell cat, named after his departed third wife, Roberta.

Nora had asked him what he was willing to pay for my services. Vise responded with the magic words, "Money is no object." Nora recommended me highly. He called me and the deal was made. All he told me was that once in a while little Roberta acted "peculiar."

"Peculiar, as in violent?" I asked warily. "You mean she bites? She claws? Hates strangers?"

"No, no," he said. "Nothing like that. She's just . . . peculiar."

My first visit to Roberta went just fine. She couldn't have been sweeter.

The second time was even better. She loved the paper airplanes I made for her, and she even ate some of her dry food right out of my hand.

But the third session was a disaster.

I was just about to leave Vise's apartment, when I saw Roberta glaring at me from inside the fireplace.

"Roberta!" I scolded. "You get out of there this minute!"

She strolled out, throwing a devilish look my way.

Then, in a single bound, she was up on the fireplace mantel. She reached out delicately with one paw and sent a framed photograph of one of Joseph Vise's ex-wives smashing to the hearth, glass flying every which way.

Next she ran into the bathroom and began crazily unraveling the toilet paper.

Eluding my grasp, Roberta raced back to the living room and viciously swatted a green glass vase filled with fresh flowers off the plant stand.

Then, suddenly spent, she lay down on her back, all four legs in the air, and promptly went to sleep.

I stood there in a kind of shock.

This was what "peculiar" meant to Joseph Vise?

He didn't seem surprised when I called him in Toronto to report on the carnage. He merely assumed his Mafia godfather voice and said, "It is time to do something about Roberta. I warned her. She shows me no respect."

And that is how I ended up in that cab, that morning, with that cat.

I was taking her to her first session with the eminent animal psychologist Wilma Tedescu.

Mr. Vise had assured me that Mrs. Tedescu was

very good—and, not incidentally, very expensive. The procedure she followed was this: the pet owner had to be interviewed once by her alone, and once along with the troubled feline. Vise had already gone through the two processes.

After the therapy commenced, Vise told me melodramatically, it would be Wilma and Roberta alone.

As to her treatment methods, they were not known to Vise, except that she relied heavily on playing with the cat in various ways and with various objects.

Now, I have no feelings one way or the other about animal psychologists. Or are they called feline therapists?

I did once read and thoroughly enjoy an impressive book by a canine therapist who used what she called the "secret language of dogs" to treat neurotic dogs in Hollywood very successfully.

In short, I maintained an open mind. And I was sympathetic to Joseph Vise's plight.

After all, I did have a borderline psychotic at home. Pancho, my old gray alley cat, spent his entire waking life fleeing from imaginary enemies. It was the consensus that Pancho was a nut. But I love him like crazy.

Tony Basillio, my ex-boyfriend, once suggested a nutritional therapy for Pancho. "Give him," he said, "an unplucked chicken and a bowl of buttermilk every three days."

I didn't think it would work. Surely not for Roberta.

My personal evaluation of Roberta was that she was

regressing to some infantile state. She really seemed to enjoy knocking things over for no other reason than to hear them shatter.

Obviously, she needed help.

When the taxi reached our destination, I realized that Wilma Tedescu's dwelling was not on Central Park West itself. Just west of that avenue, it was a large, ill-kempt brownstone with treacherous, crumbling steps.

Up I trudged with Roberta's carrier in tow.

There was only one bell and one mailbox. It looked as though Wilma Tedescu owned the entire building. A large Christmas wreath that had seen better days had been fastened to the door. It relieved the gloom of the crumbling facade. I stared for a moment at it. Despite its age, the wreath was clearly an expensive one, with still-fragrant berries and plastic candy canes stuck in the lower right quadrant. I liked to look at wreaths, liked the way they smelled. They helped to stabilize me during the holiday season, when my moods tend to swing wildly between elation and depression.

I rang the bell.

There was no answer.

I rang again.

Then a woman's voice boomed out through heavy static.

"Please state your name and your purpose," the voice said.

I realized it was a security check.

"My name is Alice Nestleton, and I've brought Joseph Vise's cat Roberta for . . ."

I stopped there, stuck. It was too early in the morning. The only word I could think of was *therapy*, and I was just too embarrassed to use it.

The bright fall wind started blowing my hair about. I thought of an acceptable synonym. "Treatment!" I blurted out triumphantly.

There was a pause.

"Please enter when you hear the buzzer and be seated."

"Yes, madam," I said under my breath, mocking the stentorian voice.

The buzzer went off. I pushed through the heavy door, stepped inside, and let it bang shut behind me.

I had entered a hallway. At the end of it, I could see a kitchen. To the left was a staircase. To the right was a sitting room with a sofa, a few chairs, and a large magazine rack. On the walls were prints of jungle cats—jaguars, ocelots, civets.

I carried Roberta into the sitting room.

I heard muffled voices off somewhere.

On the other side of the room was a half-open door.

Through it, I could see Wilma Tedescu's profile. She was seated in a chair, talking to someone I could not see . . . presumably a person, not a cat.

I realized she was probably conducting one of those interviews Joseph Vise had told me about. And it was she who had activated the intercom when I rang the outside bell.

I could see that, even in profile, she was a large woman. I understood why Vise had characterized her as a middle-aged Valkyrie.

I looked at my watch. We were a few minutes early. I sat down on the sofa with the carrier next to me.

"Be patient, Roberta," I counseled.

Roberta gave me one of those feline groans that bubbles up from the stomach. When my own cat Bushy makes that sound it usually means he's about to heave up his breakfast. I was hoping Roberta's rumblings merely signaled her unhappiness at being confined in a strange place.

I sat back, trying not to eavesdrop but catching disjointed parts of the conversation going on in the office. Wilma Tedescu seemed to be doing all the talking. I couldn't make out exactly what she was saying . . . something about cats and furniture . . . but she had a very pleasant voice with a trace of a Southern accent.

My thoughts went back to poor Roberta, who was shifting about in her box.

"There's nothing to be frightened of, kid," I whispered. "No needles, no clippers, no pills, no X rays. This is not a vet's office. Understand?"

She looked at me balefully.

"The nice lady is just going to talk to you . . . put some sense into you."

Roberta turned away from me dismissively.

"Don't be like that," I said. "You can't just go around knocking photographs off mantelpieces," I warned her. "It's just no way for a lady like you to behave."

Not when *I'm* cat-sitting for you, I thought.

I plucked a magazine out of the rack. It was an old *New Yorker*. I looked at the cartoons.

Next I studied the photographs of a carnival in Martinique in *National Geographic*.

Then I read a recipe for Cajun coleslaw in *Redbook*.

Undoable! I had to chuckle at the image of myself attempting to prepare that dish.

I looked at my watch. It was five minutes past seven.

Another ten minutes passed. I started getting very agitated.

But the woman was still talking. Had she forgotten that we were there? Well, I wasn't going to let poor Roberta suffer anymore, so I opened up the carrier and peculiar little Roberta ambled out. Now, let's face facts. There is nothing on God's green earth as elegant as a cat stepping out of a carrier. There just isn't. Roberta shook herself a bit and then settled next to me on the couch.

By 7:25 I knew it was time to say something. I cautioned Roberta to cause no trouble, stood up, and walked to the door.

I heard all the magazines hit the floor, but I didn't bother to turn around to remonstrate with the cat.

I knocked on the office door, and when there was no answer I stuck my head in. "Excuse me."

Wilma Tedescu didn't turn around. In fact, she paid no mind at all to the interruption.

Then, to my amazement, I realized that Wilma was completely alone in the room. The chair I had assumed was occupied by a client was absolutely empty.

And Wilma wasn't speaking. The words I had been listening to were coming from a tape recorder in the open top drawer of her desk.

I walked to the front of her chair so that I could face her foursquare. She still hadn't said a word.

It took about five seconds to realize that she never would. She was dead. There was a small, oh, ever so small trickle of blood coming from beneath her right ear . . . where the bullet had entered.

For some reason I called out: "Roberta, come in here."

And believe it or not, the little rascal ambled in.

Yes, the woman was a Valkyrie. I could see that clearly, even as she sat dead in the chair. She was wearing a long blue dress with a small checked apron over it. Maybe her last thoughts had been about what to make for breakfast.

I didn't scream. I didn't panic. I just reached down into the drawer and turned off the recorder.

Then I picked Roberta up in my arms and hugged her.

Chapter 2

I'd been here before.

Oh, I don't mean that I'd ever been in Wilma Tedescu's waiting room before that morning. I just mean that being at the scene of a disaster . . . a tragedy . . . a murder . . . was in no way new to me.

And the police detectives who came to survey the carnage and ask the same old questions—they gave me that same sense of déjà vu.

The names change, but the routine rarely does.

The forensics team was finishing up their work in the adjoining room.

The homicide detectives interrogating me this time—Detectives Rush and Morrow—put me in mind of a comedy team. They were rather like a grim version of Laurel and Hardy.

The first one, Rush, was serenely rotund, with lovely manners; the other, Morrow, tall and haggard. He never ceased his nervous circling of the room, picking up stray papers, peering searchingly at me, at Roberta, at the walls and doors.

Rush had the mellifluous voice of an old-time radio announcer.

"Would you like some coffee?" he asked. "We got extras from the deli."

He didn't wait for an answer, didn't hear me say no, thanks. "Get Miss Nestleton some coffee, will you," he told his partner.

Detective Rush waited until the paper cup was set before me and I had dutifully removed the plastic lid before he went on.

"Can you go over that once more?" he asked in his honeyed tones.

I told the story again. Start to finish.

Rush stared at his lapel as I spoke, as if a flower that had once been there had vanished mysteriously.

When I finished he asked, "Are you sure it was Wilma Tedescu's voice on the intercom when you were buzzed in?"

"No. I *assumed* it was. I had never met the woman before. I had no idea what she sounded like."

"And you heard no shot fired? No other voice or commotion over the intercom?"

"No. It was mostly just static."

"And you were sitting where you are sitting now, for

a long time, staring at a dead woman through an open door . . . and you had no idea she was dead?"

"Correct."

Morrow did one of his little dances around the room.

"I thought she was interviewing someone," I explained. "A cat owner. Someone told me she conducted preliminary interviews with the owner before meeting the cat."

"You mean you thought the recording was a live voice?"

"Yes."

"Guess it turned out to be Memorex, huh?" Morrow joked. "You know—'Is it live . . . or is it Memorex?' "

I barely cracked a smile.

It must not have looked like a smile at all. My expression must have made me look as if I were ill.

"Are you feeling all right, Miss Nestleton?" Rush asked.

"Actually, I'm a bit shaky. This was the last thing in the world I expected to happen. At least not before Christmas. You know, peace and love and all that."

"We have some more questions. But they can wait until tomorrow."

Morrow added with fake solicitude, "You are available tomorrow, aren't you, Miss Nestleton? I mean, we wouldn't want to keep you from anything more important."

"For you, Detective, I will make the time."

An appointment was made for the next morning. I said I'd meet the two of them in a diner on Hudson Street, near my loft.

They drove me downtown so that I could return Roberta to Joseph Vise's apartment. I sat up front, next to Morrow, the cat carrier between us on the seat.

During the ride, he finally asked a question: "What does a cat therapist really do?"

I shrugged. "Interpret dreams?"

My answer must have intrigued him. He appeared to be thinking about it.

On the backseat, Detective Rush rolled his eyes heavenward.

I sat alone in my loft. It was quiet inside. Quiet outside. The "normal" people were at work. The shut-ins were just settling down for the day's soap operas and talk shows.

And then there was me.

I'd walked in on an early-morning murder.

Well, at least the day couldn't get any worse.

I could have gone back out to do the shopping. I could have called a friend. I could have found an early movie—anything to take my mind off what had happened.

I didn't do any of those things, though.

I opened my exercise mat on the floor, lay down, gathered Bushy and Pancho, and held my cats close.

I was hoping that the soft late morning sun would

cure the headache that was crawling up the back of my skull like a scorpion.

I met the two detectives as requested the following morning.

The doorway of the classic greasy-spoon diner was draped with Christmas tree lights, but they had not yet been plugged in. On each table was a little Santa Claus fashioned from dingy red velvet and pipe cleaners.

We sat in a booth and ordered breakfast.

Detective Rush got into an absurd altercation with the waiter. He had ordered one poached egg on but-tered wheat toast. The waiter had brought the toast dry with butter on the side.

Rush sent the dish back, demanding that the cook toast a fresh slice of bread and butter it. Furthermore, he cautioned, the egg yolk had better not arrive broken.

I looked over at the Puerto Rican short-order cook, who was standing at the grill with a spatula in one hand, wielding it like a samurai's weapon.

When the crisis was resolved, Rush asked me to go through my story again. I did so.

Then he asked, "You are a cat-sitter, aren't you?"

"On occasion."

"Did you ever recommend Wilma Tedescu to any of your clients?"

"No."

"And you never met her or spoke to her before?"

"I told you. Never."

There was a pause in the conversation as Detective Rush stirred sugar into his coffee.

Morrow took the opportunity to ask a question of his own.

"You're a beautiful woman," he said, picking through the shambles of his western omelet.

"Thank you, Detective."

He leaned over the table then, looking intently into my eyes. "Call it intuition or whatever you like. But a little voice inside me says that you had some kind of relationship with Wilma Tedescu. So why don't you spell it out for us?"

His question irritated me no end. "Well, Detective, your little voice is about as out of tune as you are. The way I see it, two people can know each other in any number of ways—as friends, acquaintances, business associates, lovers, enemies, colleagues. Let me think. Have I listed all the ways? No matter. I didn't know her in any way. The first and last time I saw that poor woman, she was a corpse. As dead as the space between your ears. Now, is that enough to shut your little voice up, or should I go on?"

There was a long silence.

Rush wordlessly held out one hand toward Morrow then. "Phil," he said mildly, "let's have that photograph now—okay?"

His partner removed a small glossy from his inside pocket and placed it in Rush's hand.

"Please look at this, Miss Nestleton," Rush said, placing the photograph on the table.

It was a head-and-shoulders passport-type shot of a handsome young man.

"Do you know him?"

"No."

"Did you see him anywhere near that brownstone before you entered?"

"No."

"Are you sure?"

"I'm sure."

"My partner, Miss Nestleton, found something very strange about your statement."

I looked at Morrow.

"Tell her, Phil."

Morrow played with his fork for a bit, then spoke.

"You stated that, one, you had a clear view of the victim in her chair."

"Yes."

"And, two, that you didn't enter because you thought she was speaking to someone."

"Or someone was speaking to her."

"Okay. But you stated that she was in a conference . . . an interview . . . whatever. And it had something to do with her work . . . cat therapy."

"Yes. I thought that."

"But she was wearing an apron. Do cat therapists wear aprons when they interview clients? Four-legged or two-legged."

"I never saw the apron until I entered her office."

"Okay," Morrow said skeptically.

I looked at the photograph again.

"Who is that?"

"His name is Igal Tedescu. Rumanian. A photographer. A former member of the Rumanian Olympic basketball team. He married the dead woman about five years ago. It was one of those May-December things. He's young enough to be her son."

Morrow stopped there, as if giving me time to savor the dirty pictures his words had painted.

"Young Mr. Tedescu had left the marital residence," Rush said. "It appears they've been going through a very messy separation."

"What does that mean?" I asked Rush.

"Are you sure you never saw him?" he countered.

"Yes."

"Preliminary reports show that Wilma was shot once with a .22-calibre long pistol. A small pillow was placed between the gun barrel and her head—a makeshift silencer.

"We believe it was Igal in that office when you buzzed. That he forced Wilma to answer the intercom. That he then put on the recording, shot her, and walked out the rear door of the office the moment you entered the sitting room. That doors leads to the kitchen and out into the yard."

Then Rush picked up the photo and handed it back to Morrow.

"That's what we think happened," he added. "What we can prove is something else."

Morrow picked up my check. I wasn't impressed. All I had ordered was a toasted muffin and coffee.

Chapter 3

I was being "mothered" in, of all places, a bar.

The bar was the one at the front of my friend Nora's theater district bistro, Pal Joey.

And the mothering was being applied by Nora and Aaron Stoner.

I was immensely grateful to them.

After all, did anyone need more mothering than I did after the events of the past few days?

And who better to mother me than my good friend Nora and my current beau, the good cop Aaron Stoner?

Well, *beau* may be a bit misleading. We had been seeing a lot of each other for a while. But then we sort of stepped back to think things over. That was mostly my idea, I guess. But Aaron had not fought it. We had met during the investigation of my friend John Cerise's murder. Right in the middle of the blowup between Tony Basillio and me. Suddenly, in all the chaos, this solidly built man with his laughing eyes and quick wit—who looked as much like a history professor as a New York City cop—had been there for me to lean on. Aaron and I became lovers "on the rebound," as they say. Then I realized that it had all happened too quickly. Much too quickly. I wasn't a teenager anymore.

Anyway, that was the stage we were in now—thinking it over. It was better, however, than the final stage I had had with Tony, who seemed to consider every young actress he met to be a tactical problem in seduction.

Basillio and I were now barely on speaking terms. But the blowup had not only been over his penchant for young things—not directly, anyway. I didn't know if I could consider the status of our relationship a "stage" at all. I didn't even know if I'd ever see him again.

I stared at my glass of wine on the bar. Nora had opened the bottle just for me. She had opened it with the same gleeful enthusiasm with which she did everything. Nora was still "on"—still a trouper—even though it had been twenty years since her last role in a Broadway musical. She was still the pretty redhead who looked like Shirley MacLaine but belted like Ethel Merman. I knew the wine must be good. But I couldn't appreciate the taste just then. I might just as well have been drinking Welch's.

The place was empty. In another two hours it would start to hop and stay hopping until three or four in the morning. The Christmas decorations in the Pal Joey Bistro were already in place. Along the walls were white frosted twigs. Over the mantel of the coat-room were two lovingly handmade mechanical Santa's helpers, turning in sync every thirty seconds. There was a pretty dwarf pine tree tastefully decorated with plaid ribbons near the entrance, and its identical twin at the back of the room.

"I once walked into a beach cabana and found a double homicide," Aaron said consolingly.

"Trouble always finds you, Alice, and there's nothing you can do about it," Nora added.

They had both read the newspaper reports on the murder, seen the grim brownstone on the evening news, and heard my side of the story—from my taxi ride uptown with Roberta to my breakfast with the homicide detectives.

"Do you know those detectives?" I asked Aaron.

"One of them. Sid Rush. He's a good man."

Aaron's leg had moved over so that it touched mine. Whenever he made physical contact with me I couldn't tell whether it was sex, friendship, or compassion. It didn't really matter. It was always pleasurable.

Nora motioned to one of her waiters.

The short, stocky man rushed over with a plate of hot snacks and nuts, which he set down on the bar.

I edged the plate toward my two companions. I wasn't hungry.

"Why don't you let me make dinner for you tonight. Both of you."

"Thanks, Nora," I said, "but not tonight. It would just be wasted on me." Not a lie, but not the truth either. My niece Alison and the man she lived with, Felix, had invited me to dinner the following evening, and I just couldn't handle two dinners in two nights, given my mood. I had to choose.

Aaron gave an equally downbeat refusal. "I'm on duty tonight," he said. "You know how crazy folks get about this time of year. Somebody's bound to kill somebody—or kill themselves."

I wondered if Aaron was speaking less than the truth also.

Nora shook her finger at him. "At least you can drink your drink. Not just moon at the glass."

She turned to me. "Can you figure men? You find the corpse and he gets morbid."

Then she left to settle some dispute in the kitchen.

I glanced at Aaron. He was strange this afternoon. Quieter than usual. As if he were slipping into a depression.

"I know what's going on with you, Alice," he said suddenly.

"What do you mean?"

"You feel nothing."

"What?"

"You found a woman dead in a chair. Assassinated. Yet you felt nothing."

He was right. Damn it! He was right. But I didn't like his saying it. I didn't know how to deal with this strange lack of horror of the dead and compassion for the victim.

Oh yes, there had been some shock symptoms, but that's all.

"The hit was too surgical, Alice."

"Surgical?"

"Right. The small bullet hole behind the ear. The tiny trickle of blood. It's hard to respond. The same thing happened to me ten years ago."

"What—a woman who was murdered like that?"

"That's the strange thing, Alice. It was exactly like that. She was found in a chair with a small-calibre bullet hole behind her ear. And the murderer had used a pillow as a silencer."

"Who was she?"

"A Jane Doe. We never identified her. The name she used to sign into the dingy hotel was Jan Barber. It was a fake name. And we never found the killer."

"Was she a young woman?"

"No. About sixty."

"And you never learned anything about her?"

"Not a blessed thing. Not about her. Not about the murderer. Not about the motive. The hotel was on

Fourteenth Street. Near the river. The building burned down years ago."

I sipped the wine and reached for one of the hors d'oeuvres. Perhaps Aaron was right. Perhaps it was the surgical cleanliness of the death. Tiny hole. Very little blood. The woman sitting there as if nothing had happened.

It could be that, or it could be that I was getting older and more jaded.

Aaron put his arm around me. Sinatra began to sing. "Summer Wind." A strange song for that time of year. I felt like an orphan. Yes, I definitely needed more mothering.

The two mechanical Santa's helpers suddenly started to turn. Aaron stared at them, a sardonic little smile on his lips.

"There are two ways to look at this season in New York," he said. "One way is simply that there is a whole lot more joy. And the other way, my way, is that there are a whole lot more drunks."

Chapter 4

"I just won a bet, *chère* auntie," Alison said teasingly.

"Did you?" I said. "What bet is that?"

"On the flight back home I bet Felix that since we called you from Milan last week you had become involved in some new disaster. And sure enough, you have."

"A pretty big one, it looks like," Felix added. "Murder. About as big as they come."

I went along with their little joke, but I was just the slightest bit annoyed at them. They were laughing at me! After all, it had not been my choice to get involved in Wilma Tedescu's death.

In addition, to say I was "involved" was an understatement. My God, for a while there it looked as if the police thought I might have killed Wilma.

"Well, dear," I said crisply to Alison, "I hope the pay-off on your bet is a good one."

"It certainly is," she answered, not even noticing my tone. "Since Felix lost the bet, he has to get me—"

"Never mind that for now," he interrupted her, and it looked as if he might have been blushing under his graying beard.

How could I stay mad at the two of them? They were adorable.

They were the most delightful of odd couples: she the willowy, mercurial, golden-haired waif; he the stolid, portly, mustachioed man who everyone said looked like the old Hollywood actor Brian Donlevy.

It was through Felix's goodness that I was living in my beloved loft, just a few blocks from their Barrow Street brownstone. Felix is a psychiatrist—or was—he doesn't practice much anymore. He had bought and renovated several distressed Manhattan buildings in the eighties. Mine is the only one that has failed consistently to turn any kind of profit. So, when he got together with my niece Alison, who is more than twenty years his junior, I guess he gained in me not only an in-law but a whopping tax write-off.

Alison poured another generous helping of wine into my glass.

"We bring you greetings from a lot of old friends, Aunt Alice."

"What old friends?"

"You know, from your brief but glamorous days as a fashion icon."

"Oh. That!" I said, nearly blushing myself.

What she said was true. I had recently done a little modeling—yes, fashion modeling, of all things. It was a ridiculous scenario.

Two friends who ran a highly successful ladies' boutique had once dragooned me into doing a few ads for their clothing. After three weeks on a punitive diet, Alison and I had appeared in a series of—God, what should I call them?—young beauty/old beauty couture ads.

Looking at the ads now, I say to myself, Alice, you're no runway star, and you're no beauty anymore. Oh, I'm tall and my figure will still get by, and I've always had good legs and a head of ripe cornsilk hair that is now touched with gray. But I still look like a Miss Dairy Queen contestant at the Minnesota State Fair. As a producer once said to me, years ago when I was auditioning for a part in a Chekhov play, "Honey, when I do a revival of Oklahoma, I'll call you."

Unfortunately, that modeling adventure too had involved murder.

But there was an upside to the whole affair: Alison had been working steadily as a model ever since. She had flown all over the world in the last year, showing off high-fashion clothes from the leading lights of the fashion world and making tons of dough. Half the time, Felix accompanied her.

And when they came back from one of these jaunts, he was invariably loaded down with new toys— Japanese computers, Irish linens, French wines, you name it.

Tonight he was trying out his brand-new pasta maker, attempting to replicate some dish featuring sea urchins and an impossible-to-pronounce name.

I told them all about Joseph Vise and Roberta and poor Dr. Wilma Tedescu while the three of us got tipsy.

"Sweetheart," Felix called to my niece from the cavernous pantry, "what happened to all the aprons?"

"I don't know," Alison answered. "I suppose they're all in the clothes hamper. We've got to do a major wash."

Felix walked back into the kitchen then. "Well, okay," he said. "I guess I'll have to cook in this."

We looked down at his midsection. He was wearing a preposterous little frilly white thing around his waist. It must have been an apron left over from the last catered party he had thrown.

The three of us broke into crazy laughter.

Actually, it wasn't until we were eating the scrumptious salad Felix had made—long after he had removed the French maid's apron—that the thought hit me: apron. Small and lacy. Like something out of a naughty vaudeville sketch. A chill set in.

That apron Felix wore reminded me of the one I had seen tied around Wilma Tedescu's waist as she sat dead in her office chair.

I excused myself from the table and hurried into Felix's study to make a phone call.

I sent up a prayer that Aaron Stoner would be at home.

"Hey, Lady Bernhardt," he greeted me. "I was just thinking about you."

"Really? What were you thinking?"

"Why don't you come over. I'll tell you."

"Tempting," I said, "but I'm in the middle of dinner at Felix and Alison's place. And I just thought of something I must ask you."

"Shoot."

"Remember you told me about that old Jane Doe of yours? The unsolved case. The woman who was found in the hotel with a"—I hesitated there, and then lowered my voice a notch—"with a bullet beneath the ear. They used a pillow to muffle the sound. Just the way the cat therapist was killed."

"Yeah."

"Aaron, I want to ask a pretty strange question about that case. Was there an apron on the body? A demure little apron?"

There was a few seconds' worth of weighty silence, and then he said, again, "Yeah."

"I don't know whether I feel good or bad to hear that," I said. "I forgot to tell you the other night at Nora's. I guess I just plain forgot it, period."

"What?"

"When I found Wilma Tedescu's body, she was wearing a silly little apron."

When he responded, I caught more than a hint of reluctance and apprehension in his voice.

"You're kidding," he said.

"Do you really think I am, Aaron?"

"No."

"Don't you agree that the similarities are too great to be coincidence?"

He didn't answer for a minute.

"Aaron?"

"Okay, okay, it's more than a coincidence. It's kind of . . . weird."

"That's all it is to you? Just 'weird'?"

"That depends."

"On what?"

"On whether it gets you off and running on some wild-goose chase."

"Wild what?!"

Oh, temper, temper, Alice, I reminded myself. If you had a dollar for every time a male implied you were overreacting, you'd have—well, what would I have? Maybe not a vintage Rolls-Royce, but certainly a nice little Jeep like the drug dealers drive.

I took a deep breath and went on. "Be honest, Aaron. You're a cop. If you had found a body like that—someone killed in exactly the same manner as in a case ten years earlier—would you think it was just a weird coincidence? Would you just dismiss it?"

"What do you want me to do?" he said, not so much suspicion as resignation in his voice.

I wasted no time in telling him. "I want you to call Rush and Morrow."

"And say what? That we got another apron killing— go bring in Beaver Cleaver's mom for questioning?"

"No. Just that I want to see Wilma's office again. I want entry to the crime scene."

"Okay. And what else?"

I almost laughed. "What makes you think there's something else?"

"Was I born yesterday, Alice? I never met the woman who didn't want a two-part favor."

This time I did laugh.

"All right, Aaron. You've nailed me. Actually, it's a three-parter."

"See what I mean?"

"I'd like Rush and Morrow to let me go over the inventory of Wilma's home and office."

"Uh-huh. And what else?"

"Well, actually, you're the one who can do part three."

"Me?"

"Yes. I want you to dig up your old paperwork on the Jane Doe case and show it to me. I know it's probably a pain in the neck, but could you get on it?"

Again, there was a pause.

"Aaron, are you there?"

"I'm here. I was just thinking about how you're going to pay me back for this."

"Well, pleasant dreams, Detective Stoner. I'll talk to you tomorrow."

I walked back to the dinner table. Felix and Alison were in the midst of a tiff. I sat down and stared at my plate.

Why had I so quickly jumped back into the murder? Why had those crazy aprons made me feel that it was necessary to do something? I couldn't really articulate a rational reason. But deep down I had this funny, persistent tickle that Wilma Tedescu was dead because I had been too dim-witted to recognize a murder in progress. And this shamed me. It shamed me no end.

"Aunt Alice!"

"Yes."

"You didn't seem to hear a word I was saying to you," Alison said.

"I tuned out when I heard you and Felix arguing," I fabricated. There was no point in revealing to Alison the shame I was contemplating.

"We weren't really arguing. I was just trying to calm the lovable fool down."

"About what?"

"He's starting to shop for the Christmas tree. He gets a bigger one each year. And it has to be a balsam fir. The one he got last year couldn't even fit through the door. It was too tall. So there was all kinds of lunacy with buzz saws and hatchets. I just told him to calm down this year. He resented it."

"A lovers' quarrel," I noted.

She smiled happily.

Chapter 5

The same stately trees that a few weeks ago had sported leaves of incredible golds and greens and yellows now were almost bare. The dark and delicate branches were like so many scarecrows.

Spare and haunting, Central Park looked so glorious in the cold morning that I could barely pull myself away from the bench and cross over to Dr. Tedescu's old office. I could almost feel snow in the wind. A white Christmas was coming, I predicted.

But Detective Morrow had told me to be at the dilapidated brownstone promptly at eight. A uniformed officer would meet me then and accompany me into the house. I didn't want him—or her—to have to wait for even five seconds. So I arrived at ten before eight.

Officer Fields was forty-five minutes late. After he

checked my identification he handed me a photocopy of the inventory I had requested of Detective Morrow. Then he tipped his hat. But he offered no apologies for his tardiness. I didn't dare ask any questions or show annoyance.

While I went picking and poking all over the ground floor of Wilma Tedescu's place, the uniformed cop sat in the waiting room drinking take-out coffee and browsing through the same magazines I had looked at the morning I found Wilma's body.

When I checked out the kitchen with its antiquated fixtures, I recalled Aaron Stoner's wisecrack about Beaver Cleaver's mom. It did look like something out of the fifties in there—all rounded edges and rusting chrome handles.

But there was certainly no cache of cute little aprons in the pantry or in any of the cabinets.

In Wilma's office I found nothing out of the ordinary—standard-issue metal desk, a couple of old brown leather chairs, worn carpeting, desk lamp and calendar, pencil sharpener, file cabinet, dictionary. The telephone was a heavy old rotary-dial model.

Yes, everything seemed vaguely reminiscent of the past, so it came as no surprise that Wilma didn't own a computer. I guess she didn't hold by very many of the modern trappings of life.

Well, that wasn't altogether true. There had been the tape recorder in her desk drawer—assuming it belonged to her and not the killer.

I read through a few of the defunct client files: a gray and white male named Pickles, who was perpetually constipated because he liked to eat newspapers.

Cured in 1989.

A ginger tabby, Simon, who had discovered a way to turn on the shower and had, before he was cured three years before, cost his owner $13,000 in bathroom repairs.

A purebred Siamese who peed every time the radio went on.

Case closed in 1990.

The litany of neurotic felines—and Dr. Tedescu's cures—continued. As my old friend Tony Basillio might have observed: oh brother! These cats made my Pancho look like a model of well-adapted sanity.

I sat down at Wilma's desk and leafed through the small red notebook on the desk blotter. It was a dime-store blank book that the doctor had fashioned into a homemade appointment calendar. Patients to see, errands to run, and so on.

Curious. Two or three of the pet and owner names I had just read about kept recurring on the pages of the book.

I didn't understand. The files I had just read indicated that those cats had been cured and the cases closed out.

I turned to the current month.

I *really* didn't understand. An appointment had

been made for a certain cat who, according to the de-funct records, died a couple of years ago.

Then, when I just happened to remember that my birthday was not far away and that, as Nora had re-quested, I had to make a dinner date with her to cele-brate, I noticed that the dates in Wilma's journal were off. In other words, last Thursday had not been the tenth of the month, as Wilma had written, nor was next Thursday the twenty-fourth.

I flipped to the front of the journal.

Something had been written on page one, but heavy black ink now obscured it. I held the page up close to the lamplight, trying to see the original writing through the cross-out. At last I was able to make out what had been written there: 1988.

This appointment book was years out of date.

Someone had switched it for the real date book.

I opened a few more drawers and cabinets in the of-fice. One was filled with plastic and wood spinning tops—children's toys. Wilma must have kept these for the children of her clients. Give the kids something to play with while the family pet is with its shrink.

In another drawer I came upon a stack of home-made appointment books from the past. But not the one for this year or last.

I looked carefully at the inventory of items the police had taken away from the crime scene. There was no appointment book listed.

Someone had taken Wilma's appointment book. I had to assume that that someone was our killer.

Why would the killer want to remove Wilma's appointment books? Because his or her name was in them, obviously.

The only one of Wilma's current clients whom I knew of was actually *my client* as well: Joseph Vise. His naughty cat, Roberta, was the reason I was caught up in all this.

It seemed pretty safe to eliminate Vise as a suspect. He had a damn good alibi: when Wilma was killed, he was before the cameras in Toronto, making a kidnapped-baby–Mideastern-terrorist–disease-of-the-week TV movie.

I needed to know who Wilma's other clients had been. What was I going to do? It is at times like these that I am most sorry I don't have the magic and terrifying power—like the power of the police—to subpoena bank records or order telephone logs from the phone company.

Instead, I have to be snoopy and devious. Dishonest, is the way Tony Basillio would characterize it. We had many a fight about things like that.

I went back to rifling whatever papers I could lay my hands on, thinking that maybe I could locate some paid bills or perhaps some unmailed statements. Nothing of the kind turned up.

It was time for that inevitable stage of an investigation, the one where I sit in the nearest chair and stare into space for several minutes, hoping for inspiration. This step often includes reaching for the telephone. I never know whose number I'm going to dial. I decide after picking up the receiver.

Officer Fields came into the room just then. My time was up.

It was while I was enjoying a piece of strudel in the Bavarian café on Amsterdam Avenue that I remembered the number I had been about to dial when the uniformed cop intruded on my privacy: 411.

I paid my check and used the pay phone near the ladies' room. Information listed, not surprisingly, only one Igal Tedescu. Wilma Tedescu's estranged husband agreed to see me—but not until after a struggle. He hung up when I first told him I wanted to talk to him about the death of his wife. With my second call, after I told him that I knew he was the prime suspect in the case, he let loose with a string of what I took to be Rumanian curse words. Then he fell silent when I reminded him he could use all the friends he could get, being that he was a stranger in a strange land.

I told him it would take me a while to get downtown to his apartment in Chelsea.

I was taken aback when he scoffed. "Just go to Central Park West and take the A train," he said impatiently, as if I were a pesky tourist.

Igal answered the door in jeans and no shirt. Indeed he was younger than Wilma—a lot younger.

Was he the gigolo the police made him out to be? I guess he fit the bill sheerly from a physical point of view. But I was determined not to prejudge him.

He was dark and rangy with coal black hair and searing black eyes, a powerful torso, and a delicate waist. Then I remembered: he was a former athlete—a basketball player. The first one I had ever met. Oh, I'd seen some of them on TV or in the schoolyards. Few had been as good-looking as Igal Tedescu.

I knew he was a foreigner—a Rumanian, the police had said. But his English was close to flawless. It was only when he pronounced words such as *cops* that his accent was apparent. He was sick of the *kopes* asking him questions, making his life miserable, he said.

"Why did you call me, Miss Nestleton? How do I know you are not working in league with the police?"

"I'm not, Igal. I'm neither with them nor against them. I just want to find out who killed Wilma."

"Why are you interested in Wilma? Did she do anything to you? For you? What do you really want?"

"I know it's asking a lot to expect you to trust me," I responded. "But you don't have many options, do you?"

He did not kill his wife Wilma, Igal insisted. Yes, it was true that they were separated at the time of her murder, and that it was far from an amicable separation, but did that mean he killed her?

"No, of course not," I said.

I put on a sympathetic face—and it wasn't all pretense; I did sympathize with him somewhat, and my hunch was that he hadn't done it. My hunch was that some client whose name appeared in the missing date books was the murderer.

Now I needed to draw as much information as possible out of Igal. Perhaps if he truly believed I was not just another accuser, he would confide in me, maybe remember things he had not thought to tell the investigating detectives.

The smell of expresso was strong in the apartment. Igal led me through the sunny, skylit living room, littered here and there with bachelor detritus, and into the spacious, beautifully appointed kitchen.

I took a quick look around as I walked. Tiled fireplace. Two sleeping lofts high up on a trellised balcony. A huge marble quarry of a bathroom.

Nice place. The rent, I guessed, was no bargain.

He pulled on a yellow sweatshirt and quickly set about making fresh coffee for me.

"So it is true I don't wear black because of Wilma," Igal said after he had settled in the chair across from me. "I don't pretend to be mourning, you know?"

"Yes," I said. "Perhaps that's one of the reasons the police suspect you."

Igal gave half a sneer. "Well, I cannot help that. They don't want to take the time to find the real killer. And maybe it's not such an easy job. That Wilma was . . . well, let's just say the streets are not full of mourners for her. Nobody will miss her much except those crazy cats."

"That's a very harsh thing to say."

"It is true."

"I don't know if I believe you. A woman who can cure cats has to love them. And love transcends species."

"Don't tell me. You too are a cat worshipper, correct?"

Choosing not to get into that, I posed another question. "I take it you think Wilma was good at her work."

"She was a genius at her work. People paid her a lot of money to make their cats well. She earned it—if you believe in that sort of stuff."

"What sort of stuff do you mean?"

"Well, she had all these theories about animal behavior. Like the one about—how did she call it— instinctual prowling curiosity. Most domestic cats deal with the problem successfully. But in some the repression of the instinct has negative consequences. In short, it makes them act like nuts.

"Wilma treated these cats with simple toys— spinning tops that released blocked instincts, she said. Personally I believe she found a way to hypnotize those cats. If anybody could do that, Wilma could. I always thought she was some kind of witch."

"Some kind of what?" I asked, pretending not to have heard.

Igal's jaw relaxed a bit, and he actually laughed at my little joke.

"Only in America," he said, chuckling.

"What do you mean?" I asked.

"Who else would spend so much money on a little house pet? Who else but Americans would have so much to spend?"

"So your wife made a great deal of money?"

"Sometimes. I guess so. You'd never know it from the way we lived, though." He clucked in distaste. "We lived like pensioners. Worse. When we first married she put me on a fifty-dollar-a-week allowance, like a teenager. It was humiliating.

"Everyone used to think that Wilma had done a good deed marrying a poor Rumanian. Like I was a little savage with no shoes. But listen—in 1988 I was on the Rumanian national basketball team. Rumania was still Communist then. The Communists treated athletes like princes. I lived very well, thank you. Then I defected. On a tour, in Canada. Not because I was poor but because I wanted freedom to do my art—my photography. And even if I hadn't married Wilma, I would have become a citizen. I claimed political asylum and I would have gotten it. All defecting athletes got it in those days.

"Do you know that it wouldn't have mattered if Wilma was pulling in a million dollars a week? She held on to her money like a drowning man with a raft. She must have been making it by the carload, yet she bought day-old bread and supermarket meat that looked like shoe leather. She was the cheapest, stingiest cow you can imagine."

He stopped for a moment and seemed to be looking for a cigarette. I knew there was probably a lot of special pleading in his defensive monologue. And a lot of delusions. He continued: "You saw the house for yourself. The steps needed repairing. The plumbing was falling apart. When I told Wilma the cleaning woman was going to quit unless we got a new vacuum, she sent me to Macy's with twenty-nine dollars. Twenty-nine dollars!"

Igal shook his head then. "I don't know," he added philosophically. "Wilma was crazy like a loon. But those clients of hers had to be just as crazy."

"Did you know any of her clients personally?"

"Not really. I saw a few of them coming and going from the house. The regulars. But in the last couple of years there haven't really been many clients."

"You mean her practice wasn't doing very well?"

He shrugged. "Maybe people are getting smarter about throwing their money around. Or maybe they don't have so much of it to throw these days. Anyway, I don't think there were more than three or four patients left."

"Three or four patients," I repeated. "Do you mean the cats or the owners?"

"I meant the cats," Igal's lips curled. "Overpampered, neurotic little creatures. But then, where would they be without the fools with the checkbooks?"

"Do you really think so little of people who love their animals, Igal?"

"I suppose it's their business what they do with their money," he said. "They weren't all bad anyway."

"So you do know some of the clients personally?"

"Yes," he said reluctantly. "One or two. Wilma and I went to dinner once at the home of a couple—the Tanners. Arty types with a lot of money. Down near Wall Street. I suppose they were nice enough."

"Anyone else?" I prodded, taking out my small yellow notepad and pen.

"Well, Rita Falco is nice. I met her a few times in the reception room. I had coffee with her, I think . . . once or twice. But that was a while ago."

"Where does Rita live?"

"I don't really recall," he said dismissively. "I told you, we only spoke in the reception room and went out for coffee while her cat was in with Wilma."

"Anyone else you can remember seeing or hearing about?"

He considered my question for a minute.

"Oh yes. That funny young fellow. An actor. Not an actor, really. He is a comedian. One sees him from time to time on the TV."

"Do you know his name?"

"I think it's something like the old cartoon character."

"What cartoon?"

"Oh, you know. The one with the mouse."

"You don't mean Mickey Mouse!" I asked in astonishment.

"Mickey. Yes, that is the first name. As for his last name, I cannot recall it. Ask someone who knows more about those things. I think he is popular in America."

Despite my prompting, he couldn't remember any other clients at the moment.

I finished my coffee and thanked him for his time. I wondered what he would say to me if he knew Wilma might still be alive if I had had even the slightest suspicion that something was amiss in that dreary house on that terrible morning.

"You really do have a lovely place here," I said as he showed me out.

"Thank you, but it isn't mine."

"Oh?" I said, expecting him to elaborate.

But he didn't.

Igal Tedescu seemed to think about money a lot. Maybe too much. While it was my belief that the murderer of Wilma Tedescu was one of her clients, I also knew it would be foolish to rule Igal out as the killer.

Wilma and Igal had been separated, but not yet divorced. If she had been a cheapskate who was socking away money for years, then Igal stood to inherit it all, along with any property or investments she had.

Maybe, just maybe, the *kopes* weren't wrong this time.

Chapter 6

"His name is Mickey Repp. Don't you ever watch the *Tonight* show?"

"No," I answered Joseph Vise's question sheepishly.

I don't know why, but I almost felt ashamed at having to say no to him—as if I was letting him down. He could have that effect on people. I guess it came from playing so many biblical characters.

Mr. Vise was back from the Toronto shoot. He found Roberta in fine fettle, he said. She was being as sweet as pie—for the moment.

My guess was that kitty was sitting in his lap as he spoke to me on the phone, because I could hear him murmur something goofy like "Say hello to Alice," and then the cat's obedient meowing.

I had filled him in on the happenings of the last

couple of days and explained why he and his troubled cat were going to have to find another shrink.

I found myself relating events in minute detail, maybe not so much for his benefit as to clarify my own thoughts and the extent of my nagging guilt. He was a good audience. I had ended the story with my visit to Igal Tedescu and his faulty memory about the comic named Mickey.

"I'm not much of a sleeper anymore," Vise said. "I've become an insomniac in my old age. I'm up till all hours watching the tube. You see Mickey Repp on the talk shows. The kid's got something. He's not bad."

Supplying Mickey's last name wasn't Vise's only good turn. He also knew of another of Wilma Tedescu's clients—two clients, actually; they were a married couple. Raymond and Christine Dunn.

"They run the fancy-schmancy housewares store on Fifth Avenue. They've got four stores in the city, as a matter of fact. And they keep a cat in each one. The big tomcat at the Fifth Avenue store is cuckoo. That's why they took him to Wilma. She was fixing him up."

Before he hung up, Joseph Vise thanked me for taking such good care of Roberta and assured me my check would be in the mail tomorrow.

"Thank you," I said. "By the way, how was the movie?"

"How are any of them?" he retorted. "They're all crap."

* * *

Over near the French cookware, a huge, rust-colored cat with a tail like a feather duster was delicately eating chopped liver from a martini glass.

Love at first sight! I wanted to pick him up and carry him to my castle.

Surely this cat had never been "cuckoo," as Joseph Vise had so flippantly put it.

"Ready for dessert, Sarge?"

The question came from a trim woman in her forties. She was clad in painter's overalls and a man's crisp white shirt with rolled-up sleeves.

The big cat answered by placing his nose on hers and cooing like a dove.

Jealous, I watched their little lovefest. I must have been grinning like an idiot.

"I'll bet you're Miss Nestleton," the woman said, turning to me.

"Yes," I said. "Call me Alice, please."

"Hi. I'm Chris Dunn. Joe Vise called my husband, Raymond. He said you'd be dropping by."

She had a strong handshake and there was a hint of New England in her voice. The pockets of Mrs. Dunn's overalls were overflowing with candy canes and green and red crepe paper. No doubt she was beginning to design her Christmas display window.

"Sorry to bother you while you're working," I said.

"It's no trouble. Here, let me introduce you to Sarge. I think he's finished with his repast now."

I approached him softly, though what I wanted to do was bury my face in all that red fur and inhale him.

"Pleased to meet you, Sarge," I said.

The cat stretched his limousine of a body out on the shelf, offering his belly to me. I ravaged him while Christine Dunn looked on beatifically.

After a few minutes Christine Dunn led me over to a counter where some newfangled waffle iron was displayed as the special of the week.

"So how are you dealing with it?" she said, her voice full of concern. "I mean, finding Wilma like that. It must have been horrible."

"Horrible enough," I replied.

"Joe says you want to talk to Wilma's clients."

"That's right. What can you tell me about her and her treatments? Was she helping Sarge with his problems—whatever they were?"

"She was wonderful," Chris answered quickly, almost as if she were defending Wilma against an attack on her character. "I don't know what we would have done without her."

"What exactly is wrong with Sarge? He seems like such a lamb."

"Oh, he is," she said. "He is a lamb. Sarge just has some—how do I say this—some gender issues. You see, he goes out at night. On his rounds. And in the morning we're presented with a batch of kittens."

"Did you say kittens?"

"Yes. He rounds up these little things and brings

them home. And he actually tries to nurse them. He thinks he's a mom rather than a dad. Isn't it amazing?"

She bent down then and stroked Sarge, who was snaking around her ankles, pulling at the laces of her spotless tan espadrilles.

"So Wilma was making a man out of him?" I said.

Chris laughed heartily. "That's a good way of putting it, I suppose."

"Forgive me for bringing it up," I said, "but I understand that Wilma charged quite a lot of money for her treatments."

"To be sure."

"Do you think she was worth it?"

"Every dime."

"And what about Wilma as a person? Did you find her warm, sympathetic, friendly . . . whatever?"

"Hmmm. That's harder to answer. I don't know much about her as a person. She was always perfectly civil to us, but Sarge was her main interest. It wasn't easy to get a reading on what she was like."

She ran her hands quickly through her light red hair and half smiled. "I do remember that I had to caution Ray not to use his nickname for her when we dropped Sarge off for his sessions."

"What nickname was that?" I asked.

"Morticia," she answered with an indulgent giggle. "Ray said he thought Wilma was like the mother in the Addams family. You know—spooky."

"Well, she was!"

The man who walked up behind Christine Dunn and encircled her waist looked as if he might be fresh from the tennis court or a vigorous morning game of handball at the local health club. He was fairly bursting with good health, all white teeth and sculpted biceps in his Lacoste polo shirt.

"Ray, this is Alice Nestleton," his wife said, running her fingers up and down the arm that held her.

He too had a reassuring iron grip for a handshake.

I questioned the two of them for a few minutes more, until a young woman in a black Lycra outfit interrupted us to inquire about the price of a juicer.

Chris went off to wait on her, and in another minute or two I said my good-bye to Raymond Dunn.

He swept the sexually confused Sarge up in his capable, downy arms and told me how good it had been to meet me.

The Dunns seemed like nice people. Terminally nice. Terminally attractive. Terminally normal.

Jeez. I couldn't wait to get away from them.

If these people killed Wilma Tedescu, they were on the way to becoming serial killers. Because they were going to bore all their fellow inmates to death.

I had a strange sort of out-of-nowhere thought as I walked slowly up Fifth Avenue. In fact, it made me smile.

But it made me want to cry a little too.

I wondered what rude things Tony Basillio would have to say about the Dunns and their multisexual cat.

But that was the way thoughts about Basillio came to me—at funny, unexpected times. Watching a movie. Waiting for a cab.

I hadn't seen him in months. And I didn't know whether our last fight spelled the end of our long and stormy friendship. We were both just letting it hang where it was. In limbo.

True, we spoke every now and then. He was still living in my old apartment, which I had sublet to him when I moved into the downtown loft.

True, we had come to a kind of shaky peace after that last fight. So it wasn't as if we were enemies.

But there was still this soreness about the relationship. Like a new bruise. And even though I had never felt the raging passion for Basillio that I'd known for other men in my life, sometimes when I thought of him—thought that I'd never see him again—it felt almost as if my heart would burst.

I was so lost in my thoughts that I had walked several blocks past the discount liquor store where I had planned to stock up on bargain wines.

I turned east on Twenty-third Street and went into the first café I spotted. I needed a cup of something. While the young waiter was making my café mocha, I got up to make a call.

The Information operator—once again—took a hand in things.

When I asked for a listing for Rita Falco, I was given two choices. First, there was a business listing for Rita Falco, theatrical costumer, at an address in the theater district. And there was a second listing, a residence, with a 718 area code. The address was in Queens.

I took them both down.

Then I dropped my quarter into the slot and waited while the line rang.

It was not Rita Falco's number that I dialed. And it was not Rita Falco who answered.

No. It was Tony Basillio's voice on the other end of the line. Tony on tape. I had reached his answering machine.

"Hi," I began, and then halted there, searching my mind for words. "I'm in a café at Twenty-third and Lex and thought maybe—well, but you're not at home. So . . . I'm . . . okay . . . pretty okay, I guess. Except I'm a little . . . I don't know. I'm on an investigation. Big surprise, huh? Well, so long. Oh, by the way, it's Alice."

I drank my coffee and ordered another, and a sandwich.

Just as I was finishing the last of the spicy green olives that had garnished the sandwich, Basillio walked in.

His face was impassive and the dark glasses he wore made him look almost menacing. He didn't greet me. In fact, he said nothing at all. He simply pulled a chair out from the next table and sat down near me.

Neither of us spoke for quite a few minutes.

I broke the silence finally.

"Tony, I just tried—"

"I know," he said stonily.

And then he ripped the glasses from his face and broke into an incredibly dumb grin.

I reached for his hand at the same time that he reached for mine.

We repaired to a newly opened bar across from the cinema that ran Indian musicals.

As I said, my fate seemed to be oddly tied up with the Information operator.

If I hadn't gone to the pay phone at the precise moment that I did; if I hadn't received the information that Rita Falco was involved with the theater; if my fingers had not worked against my conscious mind and dialed Tony's number . . . well, I wouldn't have been sitting there having a beer and catching up with Basillio.

And I certainly wouldn't have discovered that Tony knew Rita Falco!

"She's a hell of a costumer," Tony said, "and a real piece of work."

"How do you mean that?"

"She's gorgeous and wild. You know, a hellcat. A kind of twisto-nympho over-the-top beyond-the-fringe kind of chick."

I tried to digest all that. It was hard to imagine one woman who was all those things—and who liked to sew.

Anyway, it was probably just Tony's tendency to exaggerate that was acting up again.

He explained how to get out to her rambling house in Forest Hills by subway. But it was really simple and quick if you took the Long Island Rail Road.

"You mean you've been to her house, Tony?" I asked, a trace of suggestiveness in my voice.

"A couple of parties, Swede," he said, playing along. "I was at a couple of her parties. Why don't I call her and say you want to interview her."

"I'd appreciate it," I said, and lifted my stein in a toast to him.

Tony and I spoke of so many things—old times, new times, the jobs he got and jobs he didn't get, my niece Alison and her career, my place in the Village. On and on.

The afternoon stretched out, and before I knew it the sky had turned blue with evening. I had to go.

Tony had asked no questions about Aaron Stoner. And God knows I wasn't going to bring him up.

"What are you getting me for Christmas?" he demanded.

"What you deserve. Zilch."

We parted with a kiss out on the sidewalk. I had the feeling he wanted to say more—maybe make another appointment to see me—but was holding back.

I know I was.

It was as if we sensed that trying to move back into our old patterns too swiftly would spoil things.

He hailed a taxi for me and kissed me again before I slid into the back. A longer kiss this time.

"Good night, Tony," I called as the cab took off.

But he didn't return my good night. He just watched me go. And he had put those dark glasses on again.

The sunporch off Rita's kitchen was a riot of red silk. Bolts of it. Scraps of it. Ribbons of it.

She might have been costuming the chorus line in a musical called *Mao!*

Red suited her too.

Rita Falco looked like a flamenco dancer. Or a glorious Gypsy of a woman in some firelit painting by Ingres or Velázquez. Cascading black curls and smoldering eyes and a vibrant olive complexion. Seduction not just in her eyes but in her every movement.

I tried not to focus on all the dippy adjectives Basillio had used in describing her—twisto, nympho, and so on. They insulted the beautiful young woman standing before me.

Except she never really stood still. She would go racing back into the kitchen or up the stairs with every other sentence. Or the telephone would ring and she would fly off to answer it.

Rita had offered me a plethora of options for refreshments—dry martini, ginger ale, oatmeal stout imported from Scotland, a funky-smelling health tea from Egypt, marijuana, Cherry Garcia ice cream.

I settled on the ginger ale. It was only eleven forty-five in the morning.

When she came in for a landing, Rita explained that her white male Angora, whose name was Bigfoot, had been a sick kitty indeed until Wilma Tedescu got her hands on him.

Bigfoot had "this thing where he disappears," as Rita put it.

I asked if she could elaborate on that.

"Wilma called it *excessive something* syndrome. See, Bigfoot would find a place to hide—and he's got dozens of them here in the house—and he'd stay there for days and days. Sometimes he wouldn't even come out to eat. I'd get scared the poor bastard was going to starve to death or something. But with Wilma's treatments, it looked as though he was almost cured. I don't know what we're supposed to do now that she's dead. It's depressing—you know?"

"And where is Bigfoot now?" I asked.

"Hiding, of course. What would you do if you saw a shrink three times a week and then suddenly she died?"

"Well—" I started.

"You'd freak, right?" Rita said. "You'd go right back to the old fucked-up behavior."

"Well, I—"

"What's his name said you were some kind of cat lady yourself."

"You mean Tony?" I asked.

"Is that his name? I guess. Anyway, when he called me he said you were asking questions about Wilma's murder and you were some kind of cat specialist too. I don't suppose you could take Bigfoot on as a patient? I mean, whenever he shows up again."

"Sorry. I'm not qualified."

"What a bummer. I need that little devil. I'm waiting to hear from this producer, see. And Bigfoot, he's my luck. Don't get me wrong. I mean, I love him for himself too. But . . . where the hell is he?"

"I'm sure he'll appear when he gets hungry enough," I said. "Try not to worry too much about him. Meanwhile, what can you tell me about Wilma?"

"She was doing a great job, I told you."

"Yes, I know. But I was asking about her as an individual, not as a—as you called her, a shrink."

"An individual?" Rita wrinkled her nose. "Who knows? At first I thought she was some kind of third-sex creature. You know, not a woman and not a man. She was built like Arnold Schwarzenegger and she wore those dorky clothes. I mean, no offense, but she made your little outfit look like something out of Audrey Hepburn's closet."

"Oh?" was all I could say. What was there about the way I dressed that made total strangers want to make fun of me?

I was wearing a perfectly respectable variation on "out-of-work-actress" winter chic: dark blue trousers, light blue sweater, black scarf, trusty old Frye boots, and a down parka that I obtained in a posh Chelsea thrift shop.

"Yeah. We didn't talk much, Wilma and me. There was an interview that she put her clients through before she saw the cat. I think mine lasted all of ten minutes. We just didn't seem to have a hell of a lot in common. But then, one day . . ."

There she paused, a slow and wicked grin pulling her full mouth this way and that.

"One day what?" I asked.

"Well, one day I got a load of that beautiful—that guy she was married to. Igal. Stupid name, but who cared."

Aha. Rita had no trouble remembering *his* name, did she?

"Igal and you got to know each other, I understand."

Rita did not respond right away. When she did, she seemed to choose her words with some care and deliberation—not the style she had shown up to this point.

"We would pass the time of day while Footsie was in with Wilma. Maybe we had a drink . . . or something . . . a couple of times. Igal didn't have a job. He had time on his hands."

I began to pose another question about Igal, but she cut me off with a firm "That's all there was to it."

"I see. Well, since you didn't know Wilma as a person, I don't suppose you'd have any idea if she had enemies. Someone who'd want to kill her."

"Enemies are funny," Rita said philosophically.

"We've all got 'em, right? Only sometimes we just don't know who they are."

I couldn't argue with that.

"Are you looking for the person who killed her?" Rita asked me.

"Not officially. But yes."

"Well, I hope you get them, dammit. If I can't find Bigfoot, I'm screwed big-time."

I could hear soothing and rather unearthly music when I stepped out of the elevator. It was emanating from the open door of the apartment at the end of the hall.

Wyatt and Leslie Tanner, the couple whom Igal had referred to as "arty," lived in Tribeca, in a renovated loft building that had once been a sewing machine factory.

Leslie was waiting for me near the elevator. She had long, shapely legs. And she must have been proud of them, because her industrial gray skirt was mighty short.

Whatever the problem with the Tanners' cat, it wasn't shyness. While Leslie Tanner was shaking hands with me, a lithe young cat, black as midnight, came slithering out the apartment door, heading straight for us.

In a flash she had jumped up on my shoulder and was purring like the motor of a Harley-Davidson.

It startled the hell out of me. But I soon recovered. I

allowed the cat to perch there, trilling and preening and looking down on her mistress from her lofty roost.

Leslie and I exchanged amused glances.

But then, suddenly, Leslie's voice turned steely. "Bratty!" she said threateningly. "Don't you dare!"

Dare what?! I thought in a panic. Was the cat about to relieve herself all down the front of my carefully assembled out-of-work-actress attire? Was I in for an expensive cleaning bill?

No.

No. Not that. I looked up at Bratty's little face and saw bloody murder in her eyes, her jaws gaping open like the portal to hell.

Bratty was about to tear off my ear!

"Get down here at once!" Leslie barked.

The cat leapt away from my shoulder and zoomed back into the loft, turning back once to laugh at the two of us.

I took a deep breath.

Leslie guided me inside.

"Please make yourself comfortable," she said. "I promise you won't be assaulted again. I'll just go get Wyatt."

It almost looked as though no one lived in the Tanners' loft. They had taken the spare look to extremes. The panoramic city view from the high, arched windows made up for that, though.

I boldly walked the length of the loft. I could see the Hudson River, the lower fringes of the Village, the twin towers of the World Trade Center, the majestic Empire State Building, and the buzzing West Side Highway. All directions.

I took a seat on the antique rolled-arm sofa in the middle of the room. But I had no sooner settled in than I heard Leslie call to me: "Why don't you come back here, Alice."

I followed the sound of her voice until I reached the interior room where she stood next to a gaunt man in jeans and a pullover.

"Hi, Alice," Wyatt greeted me, and removed a pair of oversized protective goggles from his face. He set the soldering tool he had been using on his worktable. "I'm Wyatt. Sorry I didn't come out to greet you, but we're working like mad trying to get this merchandise into the stores for the Christmas rush. Anyway, I thought you might like to see the studio."

He was right. Why wouldn't I want to see this studio? I was surrounded by fantastic jewelry.

Precious and semiprecious stones in tins. Silver and gold everywhere I looked. And, hanging from small hooks, arresting pieces of costume jewelry. Some of it traditional-looking earrings and chains, but mostly abstract, eerily beautiful pieces—brooches, necklaces, bracelets, rings.

Busy as they were, the Tanners were eager to tell me about themselves. They had met in art school some twenty years ago and started out designing wedding rings. As the years went on, they branched out, and now made one-of-a-kind pieces for an elite clientele and sold to all the fashionable jewelry and department stores in the city. In addition, they were highly respected appraisers of jewelry and decorative art.

As for their cat—I had gotten a firsthand look at the problems that had sent Bratty and her owners to Wilma Tedescu. There was no need for Leslie and Wyatt to elaborate.

"She's really acting out since Wilma died," Wyatt said worriedly. "We don't quite know what to do with her. She's a real Jekyll and Hyde. Cute and cuddly one minute, and then as snarly as an attack Doberman the next."

"Wilma seemed to think that Bratty's roots as a panther were showing," said Leslie. "I wish I knew what kind of magic she was working with those spinning tops of hers. Bratty would come out of her session as gentle as a kitten."

I nodded in sympathy. "Wilma seems to have had the touch," I said. "Talking to her clients, I get the feeling there was nothing she couldn't cure."

"She was fabulous," Leslie agreed.

"She was also a personal friend of yours?"

Wyatt seemed puzzled by my question. "Who?"

"Wilma," I said. "Weren't you friendly with her outside of her cat practice?"

"Not really," he said.

"No? I thought you had entertained her and her husband, Igal."

"Oh! That's right!" Wyatt snapped his fingers, remembering. "They were here one night for dinner. We made a party for some German business associates. Cheap old sods. Anyway, we thought Wilma and her husband might enjoy meeting them. But that was hardly one of our A-list evenings."

"Wyatt!" Leslie chastised. "What a snotty thing to say. He doesn't mean it that way, Alice."

"Right," I said.

The Tanners gave me a glass of what they probably considered B-list wine and showed me the rest of the loft.

We talked a bit more about darling Bratty, and then it was time for me to go.

"Do you have a card with you, Alice?" Leslie asked as I picked up my handbag.

"A card?"

"Yes, a business card. We're always looking for someone to take care of Bratty when we have to travel. I can't believe the coincidence that you're a cat-sitter. You'll be the first one I call when we go to Spain next month."

I couldn't get the image of Bratty's devil eyes and gaping mouth out of my mind.

"I don't think I remembered to bring any cards with me. I'll call you."

* * *

I walked home from the Tanners' place. I was distracted. Getting hungry. But not really able to focus on what I was going to eat for supper.

It was going to be a nice starry night. I could tell.

I thought about hopping on the bus and going to Nora's bistro for a drink, but then I decided against it.

On an impulse, I called Aaron at the station house. But he was out at a crime scene.

I continued walking west, toward my loft.

You know, when you're a single woman in New York, especially during the holidays, it can get depressing. You can start to feel . . . left out, friendless, even if that isn't true.

Did I really miss being married? Last year my answer would have been "No way!" But now I wasn't quite so sure. I mean, I certainly did not miss the dreadful fights and jealousies and recriminations that had marked those last days of my own marriage—ten thousand years ago.

But sometimes—and that evening was one of those times—I just wanted to come home and have someone be there. Even someone in a bad mood. Or still in his pajamas.

The trouble was, you couldn't just ask him to leave the next day, could you?

Well, the reception I got when I snapped on the light switch took me right out of that mopey state of mind.

Bushy was wild with delight at my return. He barely let me get my sweater off. In his eyes was the kind of "you're my world" look that I'd witnessed only in big sloppy dogs out with their masters on wonderful snowy evenings.

Even Pancho, haunted little paranoid that he is, joined in the tickling and frolicking for a few moments.

It was the next best thing to a surprise party.

Oh, I knew their attentions were equal parts affection and hunger, but it didn't matter just then. I went over to the cabinet and searched wildly for that white-fish-and-shrimp flavor they loved.

There was a message on my answering machine. From Alison and Felix.

Not from Alison. And not from Felix. From both of them.

They had taken turns speaking into the receiver, and then, at the end of the message, they had said, "Call us. Love you," as one.

Cute.

Oh Lord. Couples.

I fed the cats and then called out for Thai food.

When it arrived, I attacked the savory dumplings and all those piquant noodles and pork. But then I began to eat very slowly. It dawned on me that I was eating in the same slow mode that had characterized my investigation so far. I set my chopsticks aside, no longer hungry. It all felt so futile.

I looked around. The loft seemed so empty. It might be nice to have a tree this Christmas. But in the past the combination of trees and my cats had been a disaster. Bushy chewed one to death. And Pancho thought it was a big green man out to murder him. What about a plastic tree? I thought. But my grandmother would turn over in her cold Minnesota grave if I ever let one of those awful things cross my threshold.

I picked up the chopsticks and plinked out the bass line of a sad carol on the table.

Ba rump a-bump bum.

Mickey Repp was a talented stand-up comic?

Maybe.

But he was the most dour, depressed comedian I ever met in my life.

No jokes. No witticisms. He simply opened the door to his anonymous Upper East Side apartment and nodded when I identified myself.

I began to thank him for seeing me. My agent knew his agent, and so on. But he waved my explanation aside and gestured toward the brown suede sofa in his living room.

"Lola is only biding her time," he said through clenched teeth a few minutes later. "Just biding her time—plotting—until she thinks up something that will really kill me."

I looked over at Lola, a prim calico who sat washing her pretty face under the glass-top coffee table. She was surrounded by half a dozen of those overpriced cat toys I always see in the pet shop where I buy cat food.

Kill him? What on earth was he talking about?

Ah, I thought, glancing again at the sweet little cat. Now I get it. This is Mickey Repp's sense of humor at work.

But another look at Mickey's face told me that wasn't so. He wasn't putting me on. He was regarding the cat with what looked to me like genuine fear.

"What kind of things," I asked with some trepidation, "has Lola done to you in the past?"

His eyes widened.

"You don't seriously expect me to talk about that while she's sitting here!" he said, incredulous.

I didn't quite know what to say to that.

"Can you at least," I said after a minute, "say why you took her to Wilma for treatment?"

He snorted. "Isn't it obvious, man?"

Lola rose from her comfy spot under the table and came over to the sofa, where she joined me on the cushion.

She sniffed at me for a couple of seconds and then climbed into my lap.

Mickey was staring at her transfixed, shaking his head. "She's very clever . . . very, very clever," he said bitterly.

"Excuse me?"

"Oh, she thinks I think she's asleep. She thinks I'm going to say something about her. That's her tactic.

Don't you see? She's just waiting to catch me off guard."

Lola was snoring gently.

"Did you know—" I began.

"Shhh!" he interrupted, the fear back in his face.

"Mr. Repp," I went on, lowering my voice, "what did Wilma Tedescu say was wrong with Lola?"

He giggled maniacally. "Oh yeah, right. Like I'm stupid enough to tell you that."

The cat hunkered down in my lap, dreaming away.

"Forget it, Lola!" Mickey shouted at the sleeping cat. "Did you hear me—forget it! It won't work this time. You're not fooling me at all."

"Please," I said to Mickey, "if I could just ask you a question or two about Wilma."

"Yeah? Like what?"

"What did you know about her personal life? Outside of the initial interview, did you ever spend time with her? Or Igal Tedescu?"

Even before the words were out of my mouth, I knew this line of questioning would get me nowhere.

"Time? No. I don't have any time. I'm always working. She was big, Wilma. That's all I can say. But you know, in a way, I kind of dug her. She must have been a lot of woman to handle. That Igal guy was a better man than I am."

"Did you have any friends in common? Do you know of anyone who'd want to hurt her?"

He made no reply to my question.

At first I thought he hadn't heard me. And he probably hadn't. He was staring dumbly at Lola.

I looked down to see that Lola was now awake, and returning the stare.

Now Repp was smiling mysteriously at the cat and nodding his head.

That does it, I thought.

I gently nudged Lola off me and stood.

She walked casually over to Mickey and began to rub herself against his Italian loafers. He never moved. He went as stiff as a mummy in his upholstered chair.

Mickey Repp was absolutely nuts.

If I were to tell the story of my time with him to someone else, they'd say that Mickey was having a little fun with me—putting on an act. But I knew this was no act. Nobody was that good an actor. No, no, he was crazy.

Crazy as a bedbug, as my grandmother would say. Obviously, it was he, not Lola, who should have been in intensive therapy.

I gathered my things and made haste to leave.

"Oh, hey. Listen," he called to me genially as I opened the front door.

"Yes?"

"You ever go to any of the comedy clubs? Just give me a buzz and I'll leave your name at the door . . . no kidding . . . anytime."

"Sure," I said. "Thanks a lot."

The door slammed behind me. But I could hear him talking.

"Okay, babe," he said. "What'll it be—fish or chicken?"

Lola meowed.

Chapter 7

The minute I told Nora about my unplanned meeting with Tony, her imagination took flight.

Nora was convinced that the reason she had not heard from me for a couple of days was that Basillio and I had been locked away in his apartment making love and eating bad Chinese food. But Nora has a very robust imagination in regard to men. She seems to like her men in spurts. Short, passionate affairs and then adios—thanks for the memories. She is also extremely eclectic in her choices. Chefs come first, then academics—an art teacher here, a psych professor there—then silver-haired tycoon types, then delivery guys, truck drivers, and the like. Once in a blue moon, an actor. Age, marital status, bank account—all these are irrelevant. Of course, there are long periods of abstinence between the spurts, when she merely flirts. "I'm old enough to flirt all the time now," she always says.

Anyway, it took a good half hour to convince her that she was wrong.

I was relieved to get past all that, because I wanted to discuss the progress of the investigation with her. Or, more accurately, the lack of progress.

Nora could be almost maddeningly fanciful, but she could also be amazingly insightful. I thought maybe she could help me make some sense of the decidedly nutty elements of this case.

And I was right.

I had carefully read over Aaron's ten-year-old paper-work on the unsolved murder of the Jane Doe in the cheap hotel. The killing that so closely resembled the killing of Wilma Tedescu—a bullet hole beneath the ear; a pillow used as an improvised silencer; and the victim, a late-middle-aged woman, found wearing a dumb little apron.

The information in the files was pretty skimpy. Nothing had come of the leads in that case, what few leads there had been. And I was damned if I could tie it in any way to Wilma and her roster of strange clients— feline and human.

"If you ask me, the answer's a lot closer to home," Nora said.

She was wearing an apron of her own, a big white

chef's apron with ties that wrapped several times around her small frame.

It was that beautifully quiet time in the bistro: the ninety minutes or so between the crush of the after-work cocktail seekers and the onset of the dinner crowd.

I took a swig of the chestnut-colored ale she had asked me to try. It was from one of the new micro-breweries that were springing up in the city faster than I could keep up with.

"What home?" I asked.

Nora answered impatiently, "Wilma's home, of course."

"You mean you think Igal did it. Like the police think."

"Yes! It's not a very complicated thing to grasp, is it? He moved out because he couldn't take her cheapskate ways any longer. At the beginning he figured he'd out-live her and get everything she had. But he couldn't stick it out anymore. He split.

"Now he's living with—or off—someone else. But he keeps thinking about the time he put in with Wilma. Her treating him like a hired hand. And he convinces himself he's owed something. So he plans it all.

"He probably still had keys to the place. Maybe he knew you were coming with Joe Vise's cat that morn-ing. He might have been fully prepared with that tape of her voice. Or maybe he didn't know, and the tape was just a brilliant last-minute inspiration."

I mulled over what she was saying.

"Why did he steal the appointment book?" I said.

"To make it look like one of her clients did it. To lead you—or whoever—down the garden path that you're on, Alice."

"Maybe. I don't know. But Igal didn't seem that—"

I stopped there, not knowing quite how to express my feelings.

Igal didn't seem that clever? Is that what I wanted to say? Not really. Despite the cliché of the not too bright gigolo that everyone wanted to pin on him, Igal Tedescu had struck me as being quite intelligent.

Igal didn't seem like the type? Certainly I wasn't going to say that. Murderers came in all types. If anyone knew that, I did. Besides, I couldn't really get a handle on any of the people in this mess. I couldn't really pin down what "types" they were.

"I don't know, Nora. I'm having a hard time believing he not only murdered Wilma—murdered her in a brilliantly ingenious way, I might add—but then planted evidence to throw suspicion on the people who had paid her all that money."

But on second thought, perhaps that wasn't so unlikely. Igal had discussed Wilma's well-to-do clients with a certain amount of animosity, hadn't he? He had brought up the subject of money over and over again.

"Anyway," Nora insisted, "let's put the fake diary aside for a minute. I mean, after all, it could be that *nobody* took the real appointment book. Maybe there *was* no real appointment book. Maybe she had so few clients that she didn't need an appointment book anymore."

"Good point," I conceded.

"That's right. We don't know why that old book was there. Wilma might have just been looking at the old diary to find someone's telephone number or to try to drum up some new business—or something like that."

"Yes," I said. "All that is true. But—and this is a very big but—what about the apron? What about the mode of death? What are the odds that two different people would be murdered in exactly that way, ten years apart?"

"Who says Igal didn't do that one too?" she said, challenging me. "The other victim—Jane Doe—was an older woman too, wasn't she? Maybe he's got some kind of sick mother thing."

"But ten years ago he was barely out of his teens, Nora. He was probably shooting hoops and fighting acne somewhere in a Rumanian village."

I finished the mug of ale and pushed the glass away from the table edge. "It's the pattern, you see. You just can't ignore the pattern."

"Oh, pattern schmattern! So all right, he didn't kill Jane Doe. But I am here to tell you, dear Alice, that there *is* such a thing as a coincidence. There are happy coincidences. Terrible coincidences. Freaky coincidences. What would our little lives be if there weren't?"

I took that in. In fact, all Nora's points were well taken. It made me wish I'd talked to her sooner.

"Wanna hear the results of the assignment you gave me?" she said.

Assignment? What did she mean?

Then I realized what she was referring to. I had told her that morning on the phone that Tony Basillio knew Rita Falco slightly. And I had repeated what Tony said about Rita's lusty nature. I asked Nora to make a few calls to other people in the business who might know her, just to confirm or refute Tony's opinion.

"Total man-eater," Nora announced boldly. "She's had more men than *tiramisu* has calories. Which leads me to my next brilliant deduction."

"What's that?" I asked.

"Igal was boffing her . . . or vice versa."

I should have laughed at Nora for using that ridiculous frat-boy term. But I didn't.

I didn't, because I realized that she had only voiced something that had been floating around in my own mind since that morning when Rita Falco opened her door to me.

I didn't, because what Nora said made too much sense.

Igal and Rita were two highly attractive young people. They both admitted to having had drinks together . . . or coffee . . . or whatever . . . on more than one occasion. And both seemed really eager to underplay their acquaintance, to make it sound so casual as to be forgettable.

Maybe in my conviction that the key to Wilma's murder lay in the missing diary, I was the one being fanciful.

Was it realistic to think that the apple-cheeked Dunns, the housewares store entrepreneurs, might be murderers?

What about Mickey Repp? He was a lunatic, and probably his insanity worked for him in his comedy routine. But I couldn't conceive of him plotting to kill Wilma Tedescu. Not unless Lola told him to.

Did it make any more sense to think that two pros- perous middle-aged artists, Leslie and Wyatt Tanner, were the killers?

Even Rita Falco, the renowned seductress, hadn't struck me as a killer. She seemed too self-occupied and focused on her career—her luck—in the person of Bigfoot, her cat.

But if Igal was in love with her, he might have taken the decision to remove all obstacles in their way. Maybe, as Nora speculated, he felt he had waited long enough for the payoff from those unhappy years with Wilma.

Or perhaps Wilma had discovered the affair and kicked him out before he was ready to leave.

"Okay, Nora," I said. "Perhaps you're right. Maybe they were 'boffing' and maybe I'm overlooking the ex- planation that's right under my nose."

Nora gave a kind of cheer. "Yeah! Let's hear one for good old sex and greed."

She uncapped another bottle of the delicious ale and poured another glassful for me.

"What now?" she asked.

I felt a bit foolish. Had I tried to force a connection between the murders to impress Aaron Stoner? Had I refused to recognize mundane reality in order to puff myself up as an investigator?

I closed my eyes for a moment. I could see Wilma in the chair again. That silly apron at her waist. That tiny trickle of blood beneath her ear. Accept the mundane, Alice, I told myself.

"Rita is the weak link," I said.

"Will you go out to Queens again?"

"Yes."

"Should I come with you?"

"No, that's all right. I'll be calling on you for help soon enough."

Mundane. Did I say mundane? My second visit to Rita's home was far from that.

Rita did not have that carefree Gypsy look about her this time.

She was drawn and frantic-looking, her hair plaited carelessly, no makeup.

"Oh," she said when she pulled the door open. "It's you."

"I'm sorry. Were you expecting someone else?"

"No . . . yes . . . I . . . I mean, I'm not sure."

The ashtray on the sunporch was piled high with dead cigarette butts. There was cold, moldering coffee on every available surface.

I watched her move jerkily about the room for a minute before speaking. "Why are you here again?"

"I'll get to that in a moment. Rita, is something wrong?"

She looked at me with annoyance and desperation and hope and a dozen other emotions I couldn't read immediately. It was as though she were struggling with something, trying to decide whether she could trust me.

"Is something wrong?" I repeated. "Are you ill or—"

"Yes, something is wrong! He's gone!" she cried. "He's gone!"

"Who is?"

Rita began to wail then. "Bigfoot. He was taken."

She sank into a chair.

"What are you talking about, Rita?"

I knew how harsh and unsympathetic I sounded, but I was trying to make sense of what she said.

"Don't you understand English?" Rita snapped, furious at me. "He has been taken. He's gone . . . gone!"

"Taken by whom? Why?"

"I can't tell you. . . . I mean, I don't know."

"But you told me yourself, he goes into hiding. I thought that was why you sent him to Wilma."

"I lied. I had to."

She went back to weeping.

"Why did you have to lie?" I insisted.

She merely shook her head.

"Why did you have to lie, Rita? Tell me."

"Because I was afraid my cat would be hurt. I was afraid, dammit."

"You mean you know who took the cat?"

After hesitating a moment, she nodded.

"And this person took the cat as some sort of threat against you—blackmail. Is that it?"

"Yes, yes!"

"Who took him, Rita?"

"I can't tell you that."

"I think you'd better tell me, Rita. You could be in a great deal of trouble. Maybe I could help you."

"No, you can't."

"Not if you won't be honest about who took the cat. It was Igal Tedescu, wasn't it? He's the one who's threatening you."

She shook her head violently, crying. "No."

"I think he is, Rita. I think you and Igal—"

"I don't care what you think!" she exploded. "I just want you to leave me alone. Just go."

Rita would not allow me to say another word. "Just go!" she screamed. Then she planted her two hands on my back and propelled me toward the front door.

I was deposited on the sidewalk like a common drunk exiled from a cheap bar.

Well, so much for being fanciful.

Rita was lying. Scared and lying.

She was involved with Igal. She knew that he had killed Wilma.

And now he had taken Bigfoot as a warning to her to keep quiet.

Igal and Rita. In some twisted way they were just another in the parade of couples that had passed across my line of vision lately.

I didn't envy any of them.

I had not thought ahead to check the Long Island Rail Road schedule, so I just walked over to the open-air station to wait for the next commuter train back to Manhattan.

I was feeling rather lonely and friendless again. I wished I knew somebody else who lived in Queens. Someone who would take me in and offer me a nice cup of tea or something.

But Rita Falco was my only acquaintance out there. And she felt anything but friendly toward me now.

I found a bench and settled in for the long wait.

An hour later I handed the conductor my ticket and sat back in the comfortable gray seat. The car was all but empty. Most people take the subway to and from Forest Hills. But a forty-five minute roller-coaster ride on the anything-can-happen E train was the last thing I wanted right then.

Yes, *friendless* was not a bad word for how I felt.

But I also felt a bit stupid. Duped. Done in by my runaway imagination.

Missing appointment books. Aprons. Beaver Cleaver's mom. Jane Doe.

You just can't ignore the pattern, I had told Nora. Lecturing again.

My dear Alice, there is such a thing as a coincidence.

Incidence and coincidence.

I got angry at Aaron when he warned me not to go off on a wild-goose chase. But it looked as if that was exactly the kind of chase I'd been on.

I had been way off the track.

I heard the fierce-sounding whistle of the train at that moment—and didn't even laugh at my own pun.

Chapter 8

Bushy seemed to sense that the can on top of the stack was Captain's Catch, so he began to nudge me out of bed fifteen minutes earlier than usual.

The rather pleasant dream I had been having began to blur around the edges, then disappeared altogether.

I tumbled out of bed.

Captain's Catch is heavy on the sardines. The scent must carry a long way. I opened the can and heard Pancho's four feet hit the floor somewhere off in the recesses of the loft.

I put the kettle on, listened to the news, showered, and got into my linen trousers and navy blue shirt.

Over near the sink, Bushy and Pancho were polishing off their breakfast.

I stood at my window, coffee cup in hand, looking

out at the beautiful clear sky and imagining Igal
Tedescu in that lovely apartment.

What I could not imagine was where he had stashed
Bigfoot, Rita Falco's missing feline.

I lingered awhile longer before picking up the
phone.

"How are you, Igal?" I asked pleasantly.

"I am watched and hounded by the police and
pulled in for questioning at all times of the day and
night. My business is bad and I have no money. So I
am not so well, Miss Nestleton."

"I'm sorry to hear that, Igal," I said. "But I have an
invitation for you that might cheer you up a bit."

He was taken aback, apparently. There was silence
on his end of the line.

"I'd be pleased if you would be my guest for dinner
tonight," I said.

Still he did not answer.

"You see, I have a friend who is one fantastic cook.
She's offering me dinner at her restaurant, the Pal
Joey Bistro, and I was hoping you would join me."

Finally he spoke. "Why do I get the feeling this is
some kind of trick?" he said. "Why do I think you just
want to interrogate me again? And I don't even know
the reasons for your questions. You must be working
for someone. Am I right?"

When I didn't answer he continued. "But you know
us Rumanians. We're incredible restaurantgoers. We
live in restaurants in Bucharest and Jaşi. Everything

is resolved in restaurants. And the finer the dining, the finer the resolution. Besides, I'm always hungry. I accept."

"Wonderful. We'll have a great meal and just . . . talk . . . get to know each other."

"Yes. That would be fine."

I gave Igal the address of Nora's restaurant and wished him a good day.

I was determined that no one was going to make fun of the way I was dressed that night. I made a mental note to pick up my black suit from the dry cleaner's that day.

While it was true that I was going to confront Igal, I still felt obliged to give him a fair shake—some kind of last chance. And just so that I could banish that last little inch of doubt about his being the killer, I planned to spend the afternoon doing legwork on the other suspects—Wilma Tedescu's roster of clients.

Aaron Stoner had arranged an appointment for me at the hall of records with the manager of the scanning computer that integrates municipal, state, and federal information in one database for law enforcement personnel. I wanted to see if any one of the clients had a criminal record.

The first name I would search for was Mickey Repp.

Aaron's contact said she'd be happy to run computer checks on both Christine Dunn and Leslie Tanner to find out their maiden names. That way, I could search for any criminal background they might have had before their marriages.

Was I just working, being thorough? Or was I snooping, as Basillio used to call it? The truth was, they were the same thing.

I was always uncovering people's secret divorces, old bankruptcies, unpaid traffic tickets, teenage run-ins with the law, paternity suits, fights with the land-lord, and so on. It was all par for the course.

Hell, in light of my many encounters with the NYPD, there must have been a pretty fat file on me as well. No doubt, someone at some time had peeped into my recorded life, knew all about my business. That's just the way it is.

There were two or three complaints on file from dis-gruntled customers of the Dunns' housewares stores.

Practically all the parties—Wyatt Tanner, Chris Dunn, Raymond Dunn, Mickey Repp, Rita Falco, and even Igal—held driver's licenses. The single exception was Leslie Tanner, who apparently did not drive.

I found Mickey Repp's cabaret card, the authoriza-tion that until a few years ago, when the law was overturned, all entertainers who performed at estab-lishments where liquor was sold had to obtain before they could work in New York. I recalled reading about how Billie Holiday had not been permitted to sing in nightclubs back in the fifties because of her police record for heroin use.

Wilma and Igal's marriage certificate was there.

There was the vendor's license issued to the Tanners to sell their jewelry.

There was a record of a traffic accident to which Rita Falco had been a witness in 1987.

What I had before me was a chronicle of some pretty clean living, upstanding citizens. No public drunkenness. No shoplifting. No tax evasion. No lawsuits. No spitting in the subway.

When my research was done, I thanked Aaron's friend for her time and walked out of the domed municipal building along with the milling lunchtime employees.

The morning did hold one surprise: Aaron was waiting for me near the hot-dog vendor's umbrella.

We walked to the South Street Seaport and sat outdoors at a café where they served decent seafood and had an excellent view of the river.

Aaron was raised in New Orleans. He must have missed catching random glimpses of the Mississippi. I probably would if I were in his shoes. The Seaport, attractive as it is, had to be a poor substitute. I had always thought there was something artificial and prissy about it. On weekends the area turned into a refuge for young people on beer quests. I didn't know whether, as had been the case in the 1980s, desperate young Wall Streeters still came there looking for cocaine.

That set me to wondering: did bored young people with too much money still buy cocaine? Or had single-malt scotches replaced that obsession?

Oh, well. Aaron was wearing that thin Columbo-style raincoat I liked to see him in.

"You look beautiful today," he said, "but you don't look too happy. Didn't you find what you needed?"

I shrugged. "I guess I did."

"Have you solved my ten-year-old Jane Doe yet?"

I smiled ruefully. "I haven't even solved the present Jane Doe."

"Have some of these shrimp. It might help you think."

"No, thanks. I'll watch you eat."

The breeze was fresh and bracing, growing stronger every minute. I looked out at the ships for a long time, my mind somewhere else. When I turned my attention back to the table, Aaron had finished his meal and was staring at me.

"What?" I asked.

"Nothing. I was just enjoying your neck."

He reached over and tucked a few wisps of my hair behind my ear.

"Am I a mess?" I asked.

"Oh yeah. Terrible. When am I going to see you?"

"Soon," I said.

"Are you coming over for dinner this weekend?"

"Uh-huh."

He walked me to the subway, and we stood together at the turnstile until my train pulled into the station.

"You be careful with that date of yours tonight," he called as I dropped my token in the slot.

"How do you know—" I began. "Oh. Nora told you."

He laughed. "I got snitches all over town, lady. Just you mind what I said."

I nodded.

When the doors closed I looked back at the platform. But he was gone.

Well, well, well. I was turning a number of male heads. Should I be embarrassed at being pleased about that?

Actually, the skirt to my black suit is about a size too small now. It's pretty tight across the hips, and a good inch and a half shorter than I ever wear things. The four inches that my black pumps added to my five foot ten frame made me feel that I was towering over everyone else. What a weird sense of power I had as I floated through the Pal Joey Bistro.

It is true what they say about high heels. They do make your legs look nicer. I had to dig them out of the back of the closet. The shine was still like new. I hadn't worn them since Hector was a pup.

I arrived before Igal.

Nora served me a glass of wine at the bar, and we sat there having a little conference preliminary to Igal's appearance.

About ten minutes later I noticed that Nora's gaze had drifted over to the entrance to the restaurant, where the hostess's desk was located. There was a smile . . . dangerously close to a lewd smirk . . . on her lips.

"Oh, honey," she said. "Is that him?"

"It certainly is," I said, taking a quick look.

"Alice, you know I'm on your side. But I have to say here and now, I hope that kid is not guilty. It would be a shame indeed to put him behind bars."

Igal had a new haircut. Close to the head. As he neared us I could see that he was sporting a tiny earring up at the top of his right ear—a diamond stud.

He too was all in black. And his suit flattered his long, willowy build every bit as much as mine did me.

Cunning little Alice. Feline Alice. Get them to trust you and then . . . when they let their guard down . . . bang! . . . out come the claws. You pounce on your helpless prey.

I must have been thinking along those lines, sure of myself.

Igal and I had a most elegant dinner. Nora cooked it specially for us and served us personally.

It's just so damn easy to get overconfident in a situation like that:

The candlelight is having a love affair with your skin. The check is covered. And with every sip of wine you settle deeper into the sumptuous, vaguely sexual atmosphere; engaging in that kind of offhand, elliptical flirting that takes place when you know every soul in the place is admiring you . . . or your companion . . . or your prized booth near the back of the restaurant.

We started with sea scallops and roe.

Then duck breast in citron sauce with wild rice.

Vegetables like the first spring flowers. Salad consisting literally of flowers.

And, as I said, all that beautiful wine.

As Igal was raising his wineglass to his lips I saw his eyes focus on something behind me. A mask of pale fear slid over his face.

I turned abruptly to see what had frightened him. And I burst into laughter.

Two Santa Clauses had wandered in holding baskets, obviously hoping to get some contributions from diners and drinkers. Maybe they represented a legitimate charity, maybe not. One of them was very tall. Neither of them was particularly robust-looking. The tall one was ringing a tiny, muted bell.

I turned back to Igal. "Don't tell me you're afraid of Santa Claus," I said.

He was terribly embarrassed. "I just never got used to him . . . it . . . or whatever."

"Do you mean there is no Santa in Rumania?"

"There's a Saint Nicholas. There's a Father Winter. But there is no Santa Claus."

"But you do celebrate Christmas?"

"Sure. But differently. We are Eastern Orthodox. We use the Julian calendar. Until very recently Christmas was celebrated in the first week of January. But now it's a monthlong holiday. It starts on December sixth. We slaughter pigs for the coming festivities. Then, on your Christmas Eve, we give pastries as gifts. And we have big dinners and dances and bacchanals through the new year."

"Why do you give pastries?"

"They are baked in a certain shape. They symbolize"—he searched for the right word—"you know, those . . . those things . . . Pampers?"

"What!"

"The things the Christ child was wrapped in."

"Oh. Diapers?"

"More or less. Swaddling clothes—that is what they're called."

"Well, that's nice, Igal. But you ought to get used to Santa Claus. In America he's ubiquitous at Christmastime. We have tall Santas and short Santas. Fat ones and thin ones and black ones and white ones. We even have a few evil Santas. A friend of mine was once mugged by a Santa in the subway."

Our conversation was interrupted by Nora, who was ushering the duo out, claiming a "no solicitations of any kind" policy in her bistro. But we saw her put two dollars bills in their basket. The tall Santa tinkled his bell and the two left.

A strange thought came to me then. "Maybe, Igal, you looked so frightened because you really know that tall Santa."

"What are you talking about?"

"I mean, maybe you recognized him under his outfit. Perhaps he's the real Rumanian basketball star you claim to be. Maybe he's the one who deserved, and got, political asylum. Maybe your story is a complete fake—you're just another illegal alien who married an American to get instant citizenship. And maybe the small change Wilma threw you was more than you ever saw in your life."

"You have a strange sense of humor, Miss Nestleton. . . . You are making a joke, aren't you?"

I simply smiled.

It was after the salad and before the cheese board that I began to close in for the kill.

"Igal, you are a wonderful dinner partner. It makes me sorry to know you and Wilma never had evenings like this. Sorry for her."

"It's strange," he said thoughtfully. "Wilma was not very nice to me. But I feel sorry for her too. She didn't know much joy in life."

I took a few sips of wine and then said, "I suppose that in a case like that you just have to go out and find your own joys."

He looked at me but didn't answer.

"You were in a difficult position with Wilma, Igal. I want you to know I understand that."

He smiled. "Thank you. But I wonder if you do understand it."

"What do you mean—can I understand being a foreigner with no money of your own? Being dependent on someone who was a miser?"

"Well, yes . . ."

"Or did you mean something else, Igal? Were you referring to the fact that Wilma was so much older than you, and so . . . well, not the most attractive kind of woman?"

My questions had become pretty rude. I could tell that he was beginning to balk at them.

"You must have thought about it a lot before entering into a relationship with someone else. Knowing how Wilma would react if she found out."

Igal set his glass down carefully.

I never skipped a beat. "Did she find out?" I asked.

He blanched.

"Did she, Igal?" I pressed.

"Yes, I suppose she did," he said finally.

"And did you tell Rita that Wilma knew?"

There was confusion in his face now, along with embarrassment.

"Did I tell . . . who?" he asked.

"Rita," I repeated, my voice hardening. "Rita Falco."

"You mean the girl who was Wilma's client?"

"Yes, of course I mean the girl who was Wilma's client."

"But what has Rita to do with any of this?"

I had had enough of his stalling and double-talk.

"Please stop being coy, Igal," I said. "You're in love with Rita Falco. You're involved with her."

He laughed then. A sudden, eruptive laugh.

I didn't quite know what to make of it.

"Alice," he said, "you also are a marvelous dinner companion. But maybe you've had too much wine."

"Oh please. Skip the denials, Igal. You were having an affair with Rita, and you know it. But you were trapped in that terrible marriage to Wilma. And you wanted out."

"Yes, I wanted out. That is very true. But as for the rest of your story, I have no idea what you're talking about."

"Are you denying that you were sleeping with Rita Falco?"

"Yes," he said simply.

"Well, I don't believe you, Igal."

He picked up his wine and took a healthy taste of it. "Yes, I can see that you don't."

"You're going to deny killing Wilma," I said. "But I won't believe that either."

He sighed hopelessly. "So we're back to that. I knew it. That's what your dinner invitation was all about."

"I'm afraid so," I said. "We are back to that. Everything leads us back to that. You were having an affair. Maybe you left Wilma for Rita, and maybe Wilma found out and put you out of the house. Either way, you knew you'd never get a penny of Wilma's money in a divorce. She had you on adultery. And you'd been waiting a long time to get your share.

"So you killed her. I don't know if you acted alone or together with Rita. But Rita cracked. And when she threatened to tell the police, you had to stop her."

"So what did I do—murder her as well?" Igal said calmly. "Is this your way of telling me that my paramour is dead?"

"Certainly not, Igal. As you well know, Rita is not dead. But she is distraught. Because you took something of hers that she cherishes. And you're holding it over her head. You're threatening to harm her poor cat—or worse—if she says anything to anyone."

I hope someday to be able to mimic the look that came over his face at that moment. It was the very definition of astonishment.

Igal Tedescu then began to laugh. And I mean honest laughter. He roared with it, head thrown back. He upset his water glass. He slapped his thigh. He choked. He gasped for breath. He doubled over.

If every eye in the room had not been on us before, it certainly was now.

I sat there watching him, stiff as a board.

Nora—in fact the whole staff—was staring at us in a kind of fascinated horror.

At last, Igal wiped his eyes, spent.

"Finished?" I asked stonily.

He nodded, almost crazily. "Yes, madam. I think 'finished' describes my situation perfectly. I feel as if I am absolutely finished. Terminal. This is the perfect end to my absurd pilgrimage to America. I'm going to end up in prison for catnapping!"

Then the laughing erupted again. There was another minute's worth of unbridled laughter in him. When

that was over and he was composed, he faced me
soberly.

"Don't you understand *anything*? No, I can see that
you don't. Listen carefully to me, Miss Nestleton.

"I was having a great deal of difficulty obtaining the
papers to emigrate to this country. You see, the au-
thorities do a lot of investigating when a person wants
to do that. The reports on me were not very good, apparently. There seems to be nothing so despised in
your culture as a homosexual athlete.

"I gave Wilma all the money I had saved. What she
gave me was a way to stay here and become a citizen.
She married me.

"Yes, she married me. But she was in no sense my
wife. Don't you see what a ludicrous thing a real marriage between the two of us would have been, Miss
Nestleton? I have known who I was, sexually, since I
was eleven years old.

"What Wilma and I had was an arrangement—a
business arrangement. But even so, I thought there
could be some friendship, generosity, support between
us. I know a number of women—young and old—that
I'm really very fond of. And why not? They have been
extremely companionable and kind to me. But I have
no interest in their bodies. And their bodies are incal-
culably more desirable than was Wilma's.

"I didn't need a wife . . . a lover. I needed friends. I
have never had to worry about my carnal needs, Miss
Nestleton. Not when I was thirteen and not now. I was

alone in a foreign country—no family, struggling to get a business of my own going. Can you blame me for reaching out to the nice women—and men—that I met? Well, I guess you do blame me. You and the police and many others. It's so much easier to think of me as a ruthless parasite and seducer than just a lonely human being, isn't it?"

I sat in silence, trying to keep my face expressionless. I was trying desperately to fit things together in my mind. Like the pieces of a jigsaw puzzle. Taking one part of the picture and trying it out in one corner, then the opposite corner, then somewhere near the center.

I was also trying to think what I could possibly say or do if it turned out that Igal was telling the truth.

"You think I'm making all this up?" he asked with a sneer.

I managed to find my voice. "I don't know," I said.

And I meant that.

"Let me ask you something, Igal. What is the business you've been referring to? You mentioned it on the telephone and again just now. I thought Wilma was supporting you."

"As you know, I was still playing basketball when I came here," Igal said. "An athlete's working life is a short one. So I thought I had better develop the only other skill I had. I'm a photographer. Not a bad one. But not a terribly successful one, unfortunately. Still, my work brought in a bit of money over the years.

"Of course, Wilma didn't need my earnings, but she insisted that I turn most of them over to her anyway. And in addition, she always wanted my help or advice with her own photographic work. It was just another way for her to control me."

"Wait a minute, wait a minute. I don't understand," I said. "What is this about Wilma's photographic work?"

"Pho-tog-ra-phy," he reiterated, as though I were a moron. "Wilma not only made a handsome living from working with animals; she was a serious photographer too. She couldn't be bothered with going to school and taking classes or learning the basic techniques or studying the history of it, of course. She just jumped right in and started taking photographs.

"It's amazing. She was making money from that too. It's as if everything she touched turned to gold. Yet she still had us living like welfare recipients.

"It got to the point where I just didn't care about security or clothes or food or anything else. I had to get away from her.

"A lovely woman I once did some work for recently married a wealthy attorney. They've lent me their apartment while they're on an extended honeymoon. Thank God, not everybody with money is like Wilma."

I let it all sink in.

Earlier that day, everything in me—except for a mere whisper of a doubt—had said Igal was guilty of Wilma's murder.

Now the tables were turned: everything in me—

except for a mere whisper—was saying he was innocent.

The source of the doubt was Rita Falco and her missing cat. If Igal hadn't taken Bigfoot, then who had?

If it wasn't Igal's guilty secret that Rita knew, then whose?

"Excuse me," Igal said rather loudly.

I realized that he had been trying to get my attention for some time.

I looked at him.

"Yes, of course," I mumbled. "You want to get home."

"Not just yet, I don't," he said. "I believe your friend wants to know if she should serve the soufflé now."

I looked dully at Nora, who was setting the piping hot dessert down in front of us.

"Ah," I heard Igal say. "Raspberry. My favorite.

Two days later Bigfoot came home.

Rita Falco was radiant . . . ecstatic. And not just because the cat had returned.

She opened the door and threw her arms around me.

Then she stepped back and shoved into my line of vision the single biggest diamond ring I have ever seen in my life.

Rita had quarreled bitterly with the producer of the show for which she was doing the costumes.

The producer also happened to be her lover.

But there had been the inconvenience of the producer's vindictive wife.

There was a muddled story about Rita and the producer being tailed by a private detective. The wife engineering Bigfoot's disappearance. And finally the whopping amount of money the producer was settling on the wife.

But all was well now. Bigfoot was home and Rita the Gypsy was dancing on air. The costumes, she said, were going to be the single greatest achievement in theater history.

And I was going to be invited to the wedding.

Wasn't that fabulous? Rita asked rhetorically.

And wouldn't I like to share a celebratory joint with her and meet Mr. Bigfoot?

I declined the first offer and accepted the latter.

Bigfoot was a dear, goofy old gray and white thing with six toes on each paw. He was as smart as a whip and could climb his toy macramé ropes like a stuntman in a Tarzan movie.

The producer's jilted wife did hire a starving actor to kidnap Bigfoot. That much was true, Rita confirmed. But when the cat was returned he was wearing a darling rhinestone collar, groomed within an inch of his life, and two pounds heavier from all the salmon and light cream he had been treated to while a hostage.

It was clear Bigfoot was devoted to Rita. And she

obviously loved him. I believed he really was her good-luck charm.

Rita began to tell me what his real problem was—why he was seeing Wilma the cat shrink. She called the problem "Footsie's perversion."

But I stopped her. I didn't want to know.

God, I felt sorry for that cat. Forget the perversion—living with Rita Falco must have been hell.

Rita would not hear of me taking the train back to the city. She sent me home in her fiancé's limo.

I thought all day about calling Igal Tedescu to apologize.

But I never did.

I got into my robe about eight o'clock that night. Then I took the phone off the hook and opened my last bottle of red wine.

All I can recall of the remainder of that evening is taking down the wall calendar and marking off the days until Christmas. I thought about making my shopping list, but what would be the point? I couldn't afford to buy any presents.

Chapter 9

As Tony Basillio would say, You win some, you lose some.

I had lost one. And I drifted into one of my typical three-day depressions, ruminating obsessively on the lesson learned. Which was: thou shalt not be responsible for every corpse thou stumblest upon.

There were any number of limitations I had to accept. The weather had turned gray and wet, and there wasn't a damn thing I could do about that either.

I let myself go over the top of the self-indulgence hill: I ate half of a Sara Lee Bavarian cream pie, all the while conjuring up an elaborate costume drama in which I starred as Good Queen Bess.

Just about that time, Joseph Vise called.

"I'm flying to Stockholm in twelve hours," he announced breathlessly.

"That should be nice," I replied.

"I will be away for six days. But I'll be home well before Christmas."

"That should be nice."

"So?" he said impatiently.

"So?" I repeated.

"Alice, don't you get it? I want you to take care of Roberta while I'm away. You can have a little vacation as well. The apartment is yours. Charge everything—food, cleaning, booze, whatever you like. I told the doorman you'd be coming. And I'm leaving the money in the top drawer of that chest near the kitchen table. Okay?"

"What money?"

"Your fee. Cat-sitting. Roberta-sitting. Six hundred dollars. Is that enough, Alice?"

I began to chuckle crazily.

The lobby of the building was overflowing with potted poinsettias. A treacly instrumental version of "Jingle Bell Rock" was being piped in on tape. Over near the mailboxes, like an idiot sentry, a four-foot-high Rudolph made of shiny brown satin proudly displayed his cherry red nose.

I didn't know how many nights I'd stay at Vise's place. But a change of scene would be nice. It would be a good thing to get out of the loft for a while. And maybe one or two nights on their own would do Bushy and Pancho a world of good as well. When I got back, maybe they'd think twice before kicking me around.

Vise's magnificent lower Fifth Avenue apartment had just been visited by the cleaning lady, it looked like. It was ready for the *House Beautiful* cover. They still published that, didn't they?

There were nine rooms in all, including three bedrooms, two bathrooms, and a study. The latter seemed to function as the Joseph Vise museum. There were all kinds of posters, programs, photographs, and other memorabilia on the walls—mementos of his life in the theater and in the movies.

Famous people—actors, politicians, bodybuilders, whatever—cannot resist building that kind of monument to themselves. I wondered why that was. I also wondered if I'd be that way if fame came to me.

The dear old man had left a two-page list containing the names and phone numbers of about fifty food and other stores in the neighborhood at which he had charge accounts.

I studied the list in the living room, Roberta beside me, the envelope with the cash in front of me on the coffee table.

It was four in the afternoon and I was the proverbial kid in a candy store. My depression had lifted. I had six hundred big ones. And I was in the mood for company.

Why not a small party? I thought.

Everyone else was jumping the gun on Christmas celebrating. Why not join the crowd? But mine would be less a Christmas party than an I'm-over-the-blues party. Not a fruitcake or a candy cane in sight. No twinkling, blinking lights or eggnog or mistletoe. I would host an elegant afternoon do.

"Well, what do you think, Roberta? Is your party dress ironed?"

The cat blinked and started in on her facial. It occurred to me then that I'd better check all the rooms to see if she had been acting up again. I wondered if Vise had been researching new therapeutic options for her.

"Have you been behaving yourself, Roberta? Any tantrums? Any snits? Any major redecoration of the apartment?"

She yawned and rolled over. I scratched one of her ears ever so gently. There was obviously a camaraderie between us now. We had found the corpse of her shrink together, hadn't we?

I phoned Nora and Aaron to invite them to an impromptu post-depression party in my deluxe new quarters.

Nora arrived first. "Nice work if you can get it, pal," she said, looking around in admiration. "I've never been up to Joe's place before. Those residuals must be rolling in like the tide at Malibu."

Aaron arrived five minutes later. He kissed me primly on the cheek. "I hear the precinct houses in

Beverly Hills look like this," he said. "Where's the champagne?"

"It's coming," I promised.

Soon the three pizzas I'd ordered from the place on Ninth Street, called the Next Wave, arrived. Each of the boxes featured a different abstract drawing on the lid.

The champagne arrived next, delivered chilled by Joe's favorite local wine shop.

"This guy plays Mafia dons, you said?" Aaron asked.

"Right," I answered. "And dying grandfathers."

"And rabbis who double as hit men," added Nora.

"God bless him," Aaron toasted.

We tore into the cutting-edge pizzas wildly, the sage leaves and braised rabbit and sun-dried tomatoes flying every which way.

Nora said between bites, "My head waiter asked me where I was going. I told him I was going to a post-depression party. He thought I said 'postpartum.' So I bring his greetings to you, Alice, the new mother."

But in spite of their jollity, I could see that each of them, from time to time, was regarding me quizzically and intently. It was obvious they had been worried about me.

Aaron's concern was understandable—I was the only out-of-work actress he knew.

But Nora, veteran song-and-dance lady that she was, should have known better than to be worried. She should have remembered that depression in her former line of work, which is essentially still mine, is about as serious as running out of cornflakes. It simply goes with the territory.

At least neither of them even alluded to the Igal Tedescu fiasco, although they may well have thought it had triggered the depression.

When we had demolished all three pizzas, Aaron and I sat down on the huge L-shaped leather sofa.

Nora went off to inspect the premises.

Aaron slid closer to me. "So how's your mini vacation going so far?" he asked.

"Swell," I said. "Thanks for coming."

"Are you really going to live here for a couple of days?"

"I don't know."

"I've been thinking about something, Alice."

"A dangerous practice at our age, Aaron."

He didn't laugh. "About you and me taking it one step further," he went on.

I said nothing.

He took my hand. "I don't have to explain that to you, right? You know what I mean. We should stop all this being-careful nonsense. All this holding back and dancing around. I mean, I think the time has come for us to go forward, pull out all the stops, be good old-fashioned drowning lovers."

I didn't get a chance to respond. Nora was shouting as if she had just struck oil.

"Alice! You *must* come here immediately. *Immediately!*"

Aaron and I went running into the study.

"Look!" She was pointing at a photograph on the wall. "Tallulah Bankhead!"

She pointed to another one. "And look at this one! Gypsy Rose Lee. Would you believe it? See how young Joe looks there?"

Nora grabbed me by the arm and pulled me close to another photo. "Look at Joe here. And look who's standing next to him: it's a very young Barbara Bel Geddes. Do you remember her?"

"She was a bit before my time too."

Nora pulled me toward the next photo, shrieking like a banshee. "Oh my God! This one is really unbelievable!"

I turned to Aaron for help. He wasn't there. He was standing quietly about ten feet away, staring at the wall.

He was strangely transfixed, his attention riveted by one photo.

I disengaged my arm from Nora's.

"Aaron, what are you looking at?"

He didn't answer.

I walked over to him. He was staring at a photo of Joseph Vise and a group of friends at what looked like a beach party or a barbecue. There was a grand old house in the background.

"What is it, Aaron?" I asked again, beginning to get alarmed. I placed my hand gently on his shoulder.

"That woman on the right, at the edge of the photo. See her, Alice?"

"Yes. Do you know her?"

"Not really. It's Jane Doe. The woman I told you about. The woman who was murdered ten years ago in that Fourteenth Street fleabag."

Chapter 10

Something happened to Aaron Stoner after he saw that picture. He sort of wandered off. He wouldn't even return my calls for two days.

And once I got him on the phone he didn't want to talk about the Jane Doe.

He seemed to have totally forgotten about his suggestion that we plunge into our relationship like drowning lovers.

The only time he showed an interest was when I asked him if he wanted to be present in the apartment when Joseph Vise returned home from Stockholm. Someone had to ask Vise about the photo.

"You ask the questions," he said. "But I'll be there."

Nora and I discussed Aaron's strange behavior at her bistro the day before Joseph Vise returned.

"I've never known him to act like this before. He hasn't been in here in three days, and he used to drop by almost every day. After all, his precinct is just two blocks away. He doesn't even wave when he passes. I don't think he's mad at me or anything. I think it's some kind of psychic shock."

"Maybe trouble with his ex-wife?" I mused.

"I don't know. Then again, Alice, he *is* a cop."

"What does that mean?"

"He's seen a lot of terrible things. Maybe he has bad memories about that old murder case. Maybe it affected him in a strange way. I remember one or two shows I was in that turned out so bad I can't talk about them to this day. If I start remembering, I get sick."

"Possible."

We were seated at the bar. The lunch crowd was beginning to trickle in. Nora wiped away an imaginary speck from the top of the bar.

Then she said, "It's funny how that old murder keeps popping up. First with that apron and now with the photo."

"It's very odd," I agreed.

"One thing we do know is that Igal wasn't involved."

"Unless he shot her from Rumania."

"Tell me, Alice . . ."

I raised my hand. "I know what you're going to ask me, Nora. Look, just because my scenario with Rita Falco, her cat, and Igal turned out to be a ridiculous

dud, it doesn't mean Igal is innocent. It's entirely possible that he did murder his wife, even though she was
his wife in name only. Just because he wasn't sleeping
with her doesn't mean he didn't kill her."

"Yeah, you're right of course," she said after a
minute. "You know, murder is just about the most
horrible thing in the world. It's scary how often . . . I
mean, it's real easy to think about killing another person, isn't it?"

"Easy? What do you mean, Nora?"

She thought for a minute before answering me.

Nora leaned over to me then. "I have a confession to
make to you. Something that happened a long time
ago."

"Something about *Igal*?"

"No. Igal was no more than a light in his papa's eye
when this happened. This is about a man I met when I
was young, when I first came to New York. I was sling-
ing hash and waiting for the world to recognize the
next Gertrude Lawrence in yours truly. I was waitress-
ing in a steak house on Eighth Avenue. This guy was a
regular customer. An advertising man. I fell in love.
Hard. Bad. We had a steamy affair, and naturally I
thought—well, never mind what I thought would happen. The point is that, suddenly, inexplicably, he
ended it. Just cut it off. Boom—that's it. Over. He
dumped me like last night's coffee grounds.

"So, I decided to kill him."

"Are you serious, Nora?"

"Oh, I was serious all right. I was dead serious, my dear. Of course, it seems crazy now. But it's the truth. I even inquired around about a hit man. Although it would have had to be a budget hit man, because I only had eleven dollars in the bank."

"What happened?"

"I got a small part in a show. I met another man. I forgot all about it. In fact, I ran into him about a year later, and I remember wondering why the hell I ever looked twice at him, much less loved him so much that I wanted to kill him when he left me."

"The things we do—or almost do—for love," I said, shaking my head. "Lord, Nora. What a story."

"Right out of a Ginger Rogers flick, isn't it?"

"Heaven help the working girl," I said.

Joseph Vise's plane was due into Kennedy at 9 P.M. I estimated he would be back in his apartment an hour later.

Aaron, Nora, and I met up at the Knickerbocker Bar, on University Place, at 7 P.M. Only a few short blocks from Vise's apartment.

Aaron was still in his strange mood. He drank more than usual. He seemed to rue his decision to be there.

Nora too seemed to be having second thoughts. She kept remarking that she was getting to be an absentee restaurateur, what with all these mysterious goings-on.

"Joe is going to be mighty surprised when he comes

home and finds the three of us in his apartment," she said.

That irritated me. "So he'll be surprised. So what? We're not burglars. You've known him a long time from the bistro. You're the one who told him about me."

She didn't reply. She stretched and tried flirting with Aaron a bit. He stared stonily into his martini.

They were both beginning to irritate me.

What the hell was the matter with them? I hadn't forced them to accompany me. One way or another we were all tangentially tied into the murders of Wilma Tedescu and Jane Doe.

Sure, for a few days after the Igal-Rita fiasco I had washed my hands of the whole affair. I don't like to keep making a fool of myself. Who does?

But that photograph that Aaron had found in Joe's study was just too strange not to pursue.

Even if it meant nothing.

But how could it mean nothing? A woman who attends a posh beach party ends up murdered in a cheap hotel. Without a name. Ten years later another woman, a cat therapist, is killed in exactly the same manner. And the killer leaves the same signature: a ridiculous apron tied around the victim's waist. How could all that add up to nothing?

We walked very slowly to the apartment. I was beginning to experience a sense of foreboding. Maybe, I thought, my dark mood had not really lifted. Maybe the post-depression party had been premature.

When we entered the luxurious duplex, Roberta was on the sofa.

I looked quickly around the living room for any shattered objects—evidence of one of her feline psychotic episodes.

There were none.

"Way to go, Roberta," I congratulated her. "Papa's coming home today. We wouldn't want him to walk into a mess, would we?"

She gave me one of those "what a tiresome playmate you have become" glances and then turned her attention to my companions. Yes, there was no doubt that Roberta was getting weary of my twice-a-day visits. Then again, maybe she was insulted that I had decided not to stay in the apartment overnight after the first two nights of my assignment.

I checked out the whole apartment to make sure it was as spic-and-span as Joseph Vise had left it.

Nora picked up a little rag-doll mouse and began to play with Roberta on the sofa.

Aaron went back into the study to look at the photograph once more.

When he came back he sat down at the far end of the enormous leather sofa.

"Are you positive it's her?" I asked.

"It's her. Beyond a shadow of a doubt."

"I never understood why people use that phrase," Nora noted.

Aaron didn't answer.

It seemed we were all growing impatient with one another. Aaron with Nora, Nora with me, me with the two of them. Three is always a tricky number with friends.

So that we would not be forced to make conversation, I put a CD in the machine. We listened to Maria Callas sing her greatest hits.

Roberta wandered off toward the back of the apartment—preparing for a nap, if my guess was right.

Joseph Vise came home about twenty minutes earlier than expected.

And what a grand entrance the old actor made.

He was wearing a long Persian lamb coat with a black velvet collar. He reminded me of the impresario played by Anton Walbrook in the film *The Red Shoes.*

"Three of you!" he exclaimed, stepping inside the apartment and dropping his old leather touring bag. "I assume you'll be splitting the fee. Or does this mean that it takes three cat-sitters to handle my little Roberta? Where is the little vixen?"

The cat galloped into the room, the picture of innocence. Joseph swept her up and hugged her while he talked excitedly.

"You wouldn't believe what they had me doing in Stockholm. It was unbelievable. A French production company is shooting *Henry IV* for TV. They're doing it in modern dress in a Chicago gangster milieu. Sounds kind of interesting, doesn't it? But am I a performer? Am I part of the cast? *Au contraire,* my friends. My lines have absolutely nothing to do with the play. I just read reports from a Chicago newspaper they dug up from the 1920s. They picked me because French audiences recognize me as Meyer Lansky from American gangster films. Do you know how many times I played poor Meyer Lansky? But wait. It gets funnier. The director thinks I have a Chicago accent."

"At least you didn't have to machine-gun anyone," Nora said.

"You know me, Nora. I play bad men, but I'm a lover, not a fighter." Vise suddenly dropped Roberta and rushed over—as fast as mildly lecherous old men can rush—to kiss Nora and then me.

Then he turned his attention to Aaron. "Who are you?"

I introduced Aaron as an NYPD detective, adding that he was Nora's good friend and mine.

"I've seen you in the bistro," Vise said. "I'm quite sure."

"Yes, you have," Aaron agreed. "Nice to meet you."

"Are you here to arrest me for that stinking Midwestern accent I did in Stockholm? Because if you are, I'll go quietly. *That* warrants the death penalty."

I said, "I just wanted to show Aaron your beautiful apartment. We're all going out for a drink in a few minutes."

"I'd join you but I'm exhausted," he said.

I looked quickly at Aaron. He was staring straight ahead. The ball was in my court.

"One thing before we go, Joseph."

"Ah. It's Roberta, isn't it? She was bad."

"No, no. She was perfect. A gracious hostess at all times."

"Well, that's a relief. What were you going to say?"

"There's a picture in your study . . ."

"Ah, you've been in my pathetic museum. Walking down memory lane."

"Yes. Can you tell us about a woman in one of the photos? Let me point her out to you."

He nodded. We all walked into the study. I realized with chagrin that I hadn't even given the poor man time to take his coat off.

I lifted the framed photo from its hook and pointed to the woman on the extreme right.

"This one," I said. "Who is this?"

He took off his glasses, held the photo close to his face, put the glasses back on.

"You know," he said, "I can still remember lines from Odets. But faces—I'm so bad with them."

He looked at the picture again, from a different angle.

"Well," he finally said, "at least I remember *where* the photo was taken, and when. It was about twelve years ago. I had rented a beautiful summer house out on the Island, in Sagaponack, right on the dunes. It was about the time the money had really started rolling in."

He laughed. "There's something ridiculous about that, isn't there? I spent my whole life poor. And now I'll die rich doing the roles I never would have taken when I was poor."

"Do you know her name?" I pressed. "Even a first name. It's important."

He looked some more, shaking his head. "Sorry, no. I do remember her face, though—vaguely. I seem to recall she was a widow. Yes, that's right. A psychiatrist's widow. Look, my beach house was basically open to everyone. Friends of friends brought friends. Do you know what I mean? I didn't know half the people wandering around on my private beach."

He looked at the photo again . . . a long, long time.

Finally he replaced the frame on the wall and started to take off his coat. Nora helped him.

"Why are you so interested in her?" he asked.

"How long ago did you say this photograph was taken?" Aaron asked.

"Well," Joe said very slowly, "I can't be one hundred percent sure, but I think it was twelve years or so ago."

"That fits. She was murdered about ten years ago—two years after the photo was taken."

"Murdered?" Vise sat down suddenly, heavily.

"In much the same way that Wilma Tedescu was murdered," I added.

"That is horrendous," the old man said.

There was something about the way he spoke that line that made me uneasy.

A bell went off somewhere in my consciousness . . . a warning call.

This was a performance. He was delivering lines. Joseph Vise was acting.

Oh, I knew he was exhausted from his trip. I knew his body clock was out of whack from the flight. I knew he wanted us to leave.

But he was acting. He was reciting lines. No longer the crime boss, he had become the sensitive, frail old man. He was playing an old soul who had compassion for all creatures great and small, living and dead.

Witness the way he had fallen dramatically into his chair after gasping, "Murdered?" Real Victorian melodrama.

He's lying, I thought. At the very least he is covering up something. He's using this script of his to protect himself.

I didn't have time to critique his delivery of the lines or to analyze the subtext of the script.

I simply attacked.

I sat down beside him.

"Tell me, Joe, is it possible that Wilma Tedescu knew the woman in that photograph?"

"Wilma? I don't know. Anything is possible."

"Could Wilma have been at that beach party?"

"Not by my invitation. I didn't know her then. She

could have just wandered in, of course, with someone else. As I said, my house was like a motel."

"Is it possible—"

He interrupted me: "I am very tired, Alice."

"Yes, I know. I'm sorry. A minute more, Joe. Just a minute more."

"Maybe we ought to go now," Nora said.

I ignored her. "Is it possible that Wilma took this photograph, and maybe others as well?"

"What was that about a photographer?" Aaron said.

I ignored him as well.

I don't know why I hadn't mentioned the photography angle to Nora or Aaron before. It just didn't seem to matter when Igal revealed that fact to me. Now it mattered a great deal.

"All I know about Wilma is that the poor woman was a wonderful healer of wounded cats," Vise said impatiently. "That was what she was when I first met her and what she was when I last saw her. As for the photographs on my wall, I can't be expected to remember where they all came from. People have been giving me photographs for the last sixty years."

I smiled at him, walked close to the photo, and gazed at it dramatically. If the old man wanted to keep on playing roles, I might as well get into one as well. He had given me a cue. Hadn't he?

I turned slowly, pointed a finger at him, and said, "Oh. So you knew Wilma a long time. That's what you meant when you said, 'When I first met her. . . .' How long ago did you first meet her, Joseph?"

He threw up his hands in disgust.

"Who are you doing here, Alice—Inspector Clouseau? Really, you are much too attractive for the role."

"Are my questions making you that nervous, Joe?"

He broke into a grin and began to rub his jaw with both hands. "You'd think," he said, "after all those gangster parts, I'd know how to stand up under a police grilling."

I knew I had him. I had pounced correctly. I looked to Aaron for approval, reenforcement, praise. He gave me nothing.

Then Joseph Vise laughed out loud.

"Is there anything more pathetic than an old man caught in a lie?" He asked the question of no one in particular. No one answered.

"Oh, the hell with it," he said. "What is the point of lying? I'm not ashamed of anything. I didn't do anything wrong."

"So Wilma was there at the party?"

"How right you are, Alice. Yes, she was. She was at my place on the beach when that photo was taken. And for all I know she took the bloody photo herself. I just don't recall.

"You see, I was . . . we were lovers. I was between wives, if I recall. Her name was Wilma Leland then. The affair was short. And it was glorious. It was my last passionate fling. Yes, it happened about twelve years ago—give or take."

There was a hush in the study.

I waited for either Nora or Aaron to take up the questioning. But they were both silent, their faces creased with concern and compassion for the embarrassed old man.

"My last fling," Joseph Vise repeated.

"And you still can't remember the name of that woman in the beach party photo?"

"No. All I remember is that she had been a shrink's wife. And I may even be wrong about that."

"Was she seeing any of the men in the photo romantically?"

"I have no idea."

"Do you remember whether Wilma had any particular interest in cameras? Amateur photography?"

He shook his head. "No. Nothing comes to mind."

"Joe, isn't there anything else you can tell me about Wilma?"

"Like what, Alice? Wilma was a nice big girl, and we had a wonderful time. It was grand while it lasted. Things like that?"

"Anything at all."

"You mean, like did I kill her?"

"I didn't mean that at all, Joseph."

"Didn't you?" With some effort, he stood up. "It's late. It's time you people left. Unless of course the fun is really over and Detective Stoner is going to take me in."

I realized that the most lucrative cat-sitting job I ever had had just gone down the drain.

Nora went right back to Pal Joey after we left Vise's apartment.

"Why don't you buy me a cup of coffee," I suggested to Aaron.

He took a few seconds to respond. "Why not?"

We walked back to University Place and went into the very coffee bar where he and I had gone on our first date. That had been a lovely day and we'd sat at one of the sidewalk tables.

We each ordered a cappuccino and sat down at a table by the window.

"You don't usually take cinnamon in your cappuccino, do you?" Aaron asked.

"No, not always. I just felt like it. Why—does it bother you?" I retorted, not liking the edge in his voice.

He shrugged and started to play with the unopened packets of raw sugar, stacking them up, knocking them over, and restacking.

"What are you doing!" I finally asked him.

"Dexterity training."

"What's going on, Aaron?"

"Not much."

"You don't talk anymore."

"What's there to talk about?"

"Joseph Vise, for one."

"I like him."

"I mean about the affair he had with Wilma."

"Insignificant."

"Okay. But what about the fact that Wilma probably knew Jane Doe? Isn't that odd? Isn't that significant? They probably knew each other. And they died the same way, with the same stupid apron tied around them."

Aaron didn't respond. He ripped open one of the sugar packets and shook the contents into his cup.

"Talk to me, Aaron. Tell me what *is* significant."

"Do you really want to know?"

"Of course I do."

He reached across the table with his right hand and grabbed my wrist so powerfully, so fiercely, that I pulled back with a jerk to disengage it.

"You and I are significant," he said.

"I have no quarrel with that, Aaron."

"Don't you?" His eyes flared with anger.

"You obviously are very unhappy with me. Why don't you just open up, Aaron? Tell me what's wrong. Tell me what I've done to upset you."

"Let's start from the beginning, Alice."

The pedagogic tone of his voice made me a little testy.

"Fine," I said. "And after you finish I'll start from the beginning. Like why you didn't want to even question

Joseph Vise about Jane Doe. After all, it was your case, Aaron."

He waved my comment aside as if it were nonsense on many levels.

He took a deep draught of the coffee, then sat back in his chair.

"You're an actress by profession—right?"

"Right."

"A very good actress, I understand. Even a brilliant one on occasion."

"Well, thank you."

"But you don't act."

"You mean recently. That's right. It's hard to find work, Aaron. The kind of work I want to do."

"I don't buy that."

"What do you mean?"

"I think you're so obsessed with your other adventures that you don't give a damn about acting anymore. In fact, I think you don't give a damn about anything else either. Not me. Not love. Not—"

"You're talking about things you know nothing about, Aaron."

"Do you remember when I first met you?"

"Yes."

"It was all about that horrible murder of your friend. I forget his name."

"John Cerise."

"Yes. I was very proud of what you did. Let's face it.

If it hadn't have been for you, we never would have cleared that mess up."

He emptied another packet of sugar into his brew.

"And now you're caught up in another mess. And you go chasing after all kinds of crazy theories. Look, Alice, you're not a cop. You're not a P.I. And you are *not* the avenging angel for the city of New York.

"What you are is a very smart, beautiful woman who lives in a world where things are always happening. You have to learn to let the bakers bake and the writers write and the actors act. You have to stop this kind of obsessive inquiry! It takes over your whole damn life. It makes you into a very strange person. Depressions and secrets and suspicions. It poisons your whole goddamn life and makes everyone around you miserable—everyone who loves you."

The crowded, white-tiled room was utterly silent.

My legs were trembling. His outburst made me feel like I had been hit by my grandmother's old iron.

"Is there anything else?" I asked evenly.

"Damn right there is. I met your ex once. Remember? At Nora's place. At the time I thought he was a creep and you were well rid of him. Now I'm beginning to feel a kind of solidarity with him. Do you get my drift? Now I think that you might have turned him into what he has become. You're not going to do that to me, Alice."

"Is there anything else?"

"Yes," he snarled. "Do you have any money on you?"

"Plenty. From Joseph Vise."

"Good. You take a cab home, Alice. And think about things. If you really want to be with me, call me. You have my number."

He pushed his cup back, put one of the unopened sugar packets into his pocket, and walked out.

Oh yes, buster, I thought. I most certainly do have your number.

Chapter 11

I did not take a cab.

I did not wish to be in a cab. I needed to walk off what I was feeling.

I was almost numb with rage at Aaron. Yet I had held back. I hadn't blasted him for that self-righteous, know-it-all tirade he had just pulled on me.

Under other circumstances I might have gone to talk to Nora. But not that night. The truth was, I was less than thrilled with her recent behavior too.

Tony Basillio? No. That was a relationship that needed to rest. And I was especially leery of going to him with my problems with another man.

God! Everything was a big deal these days. A mess. A headache. A burden. Friends were a burden. Lovers were a burden. Ex-lovers. Clients. My own conscience. The dead. The innocent. The murdered.

Aaron.

I hadn't asked for him to walk into my life, but he had. I hadn't asked him to have those feelings for me, but there they were—along with his judgments and his damn male disapproval.

To be honest, I knew his antipathy toward my interest in Wilma's death was not just a function of old-fashioned male supremacy. It was something deeper this time. He seemed to think that in some way it diluted my affection and respect and, above all, interest in him.

Perhaps it was true. Perhaps my longtime infatuation with murder diminished everything else in my life . . . as all passions do. But it was an authentic passion—like the one I have for the theater, or my cats. Sometimes it feels more authentic, more real, than any relationship I could have with a man.

I startled myself with that admission. It upset me, even saddened me. Did it mean that I was some kind of freak?

I didn't know. Didn't every woman who took her work seriously—her passions—go through the same kind of self-examination? Didn't everybody have to make the decision not to deny who she was, alter her whole life, because of a man?

Oh, it was all making me so crazy. And it had almost killed me to sit there calmly while Aaron Stoner read me out that way and then pulled off that theatrical exit. Leaving me alone in a goddamn coffee shop!

The wind was swirling along Bleecker Street. I turned up my coat collar.

Here and there on the sidewalks were laughing couples, warm from their leisurely dinners. First dates, some of them. Others on the way home to make slow, comfortable, familiar love. I had to sidestep a band of drunks who came tripping merrily out of one of the piano bars on Grove Street, scarves and hats trailing and falling in the street.

I had little patience with any of them just then.

Oh boy. I was turning into a crab, as Grandma Nestleton would have called me.

My thoughts turned once again to Wilma and the other guests pictured at Joseph Vise's beach house. In my mind's eye I saw Wilma with the camera, telling them all to move this way or that so she could get a better shot.

There was something so eerie, so terrible about that scenario.

Imagine taking a photograph of someone who will die shortly . . . someone who'll be murdered . . . in exactly the way you will later be murdered.

Yes, there was almost an occult element to the story.

But Joseph Vise had not been able to confirm that it was Wilma who took that photo. She might well have done it, he said. But he had no memory of her having taken any special interest in photography.

Why hadn't anyone else mentioned Wilma's hobby? Particularly since Igal had also said that she made money from it.

There was nothing in Wilma's office to indicate that she was a photographer. Or in her sitting room. None of the detectives assigned to the case had mentioned it. None of the clients had mentioned it.

Very odd indeed.

Surely a cat therapist faced with lovable crazy patients would want to get a shot of the kitties. And if she was as desperate for cash all the time as Igal claimed—and as cheap—she surely would have mined this lode.

What cat owner could resist a set of glossy photographic portraits of his darling pet?

I was doing it again, wasn't I? Obsessing over the details. Just as Aaron had said. Well, that was too bad. I couldn't help it. The obsessions came along with the woman. You can't have one without the other, Aaron Stoner. That's just the price of the ticket.

I was only two blocks away from home now, and glad of it. It was close to one in the morning. I'd been walking for hours. I was tired.

When I opened the door to the loft I caught Pancho in mid-run. Framed in the light from the hallway, he looked like a trapped criminal, the searchlights blinding him. "They"—his relentless pursuers—were after him again, I figured. He disappeared before I could get to the light switch.

"Hi, cattys," I called out. "I'm home. Sorry I'm late."

Bushy shambled down from the window ledge and came up for his late-night pet and general adoration.

"Well, my friend, it's you and me in my maiden's bed tonight, huh? Like old times."

Bushy seemed to say that old times were good enough for him.

Could the gifted Wilma Tedescu have cured poor crazy Pancho? I wondered as I watched the two cats eat their late supper. Would her spinning-top treatment have been able to drive out his demons? Could she have played with Panch until he was cured? What in fact would Pancho be like if he weren't nuts? I couldn't even imagine him normal.

He kept looking over his shoulder at me. He could make a person nervous. He didn't have Bushy's handsomeness or lushness. Pancho looked like a street thug on his way to a dance.

I got into my pajamas, checked the answering machine. Nothing.

I happened to gaze out the window just then. There was a big bright three-quarter moon. Was that a moon for lovers or werewolves?

I fell asleep instantly.

The next morning I was awakened at ten minutes after eight by my agent's call.

She said that she had gotten "feelers" from a Canadian producer who was doing a TV series on the

French and Indian War. It was being scripted by a good writer. And it was a big-budget job.

I sat up. "What's the part?"

"Well," she said, "from what I was told, and this is all very tentative, you play a rather ribald laundress at a fort on the Canadian border. The series is about a family who migrates to Canada from Scotland and is swept up into the turmoil."

My head was a bit foggy.

"I thought," I replied, "that laundresses in colonial army forts were either toothless old bags or whores, or both."

There was silence on the other end. Then my agent said, "Well, I hear Lynn Redgrave was offered the part originally."

Bushy was harassing me for his food, catching his claws on the blanket and plucking at the fabric.

"Okay. Why not?" I said. "By the way, when was the washing machine invented?"

My agent let out a huge sigh, a sigh I associated more with a director who wanted to brain an actor for being a pain in the ass than with an agent. A sigh that meant, "Actors! Who can live with them?"

"I'll get back to you the minute I have more information," she said sweetly. "Gotta run, Alice."

I took a peek behind the curtains. The sky looked pretty foul. We were in for another dreary day.

I fed the cats and climbed back into bed. I didn't want to think about Aaron. I didn't want to think about a whole passel of actors faking Scottish burrs. I didn't want to think about the uneaten cream pie in the freezer. I didn't want to think about anything. But I couldn't fall asleep again.

Another thing I couldn't do was to lose an entire day to glum thoughts and inertia. I didn't know what I was going to do, but I had to do something.

Hot coffee injected a little life into me. It strengthened me enough to give me the resolve to contact Wilma's clients again. This was as good a time as any to find out what kind of photographer the dead lady really had been.

I remembered their names and I had their telephone numbers. The problem was, I couldn't remember which party had which cat.

Finally, using a pencil and paper, I was able to construct a proper grid.

Rita Falco's cat was Bigfoot.

The Dunn couple had Sarge.

Mickey Repp had Lola.

And Bratty belonged to Wyatt and Leslie Tanner.

I began making the calls. It took all morning.

Rita Falco wanted to talk about her wedding plans, but I kept leading her back to the subject at hand.

The Dunns had just opened up at the housewares store. Sarge had brought in some adorable black and whites, who were available for adoption if I could make room in my life for some beautiful kittens. I said I had to pass on the offer.

The Tanners were very excited that morning because, they said, they had just sold a garnet necklace to Faye Dunaway.

I woke Mickey Rep from a sound sleep. It took me ten minutes to convince him that we had met before—remember, I was the blond woman who visited him and Lola about two weeks ago. Oh yeah, he said, I was the one who was asking questions about "Big Wilma," the same one who spilled the vodka gimlet on Robin Williams that night at the Improv. Yes, yes, that was me, I assured him. Mickey put me on hold while he consulted Lola. Luckily, she told him it was okay to answer my questions.

So, finally, I had all my answers. Actually, they were all the same answer: No.

No, Wilma had never photographed or offered to photograph their cats.

No, she had never mentioned that she was an amateur or a professional photographer.

No, they had never seen a camera in her office.

What the hell was going on? Either Igal Tedescu was lying about the photography angle, or he was crazy. Or he was playing some kind of game with me.

But why?

I called him.

He picked up on the first ring.

"Igal?"

"Yes?"

"This is Alice Nestleton."

I heard his sharp intake of breath. And maybe a mild curse.

You'd think I'd get used to people treating me as if I were a bill collector—reacting to the sound of my voice with fear, dread, hatred. But it's not such an easy thing to get used to.

"Igal? Hello?"

"Yes, hello, Miss Nestleton. Who—or what—did I kidnap this time?"

"I just need a few minutes of your time. Could you see me today?"

"Not if it would bring about world peace."

"Aw, come on, Igal. Can't you be nice to me even for a few minutes? It's the holiday season, after all. Open your Rumanian heart a little. Forgive and forget."

"Very well. I'll look on it as a way to repay you for that fantastic meal."

"Thank you. When can I stop by?"

"No, don't. Don't stop by, please. I was on the way out to do some shopping. I'm buying shirts at Bloomingdale's. It's their annual pre-Christmas sale. Why don't we meet at Showtime? Do you know it?"

"No."

"It's a coffee shop in Bloomingdale's. On the seventh floor."

"When?"

"Well, I'm leaving now. Let's get it over with before I do the shirts. I'm hoping for another bit of entertaining theater from you. And you seem to prefer public places for that sort of thing."

"In about an hour then?" I said. If nothing else, I was getting good at not reacting to insults from the men in my life.

"Yes, an hour."

He hung up.

It had been a long time since I had been in Bloomingdale's. Not that I was any kind of expert on what stores were au courant; but I had heard from some of the fashion people that Bloomingdale's had suffered through a long period of unfashionableness. Macy's, with all its expensive little designer boutiques, had become the hip department store. But now, they said, Bloomingdale's was in again.

I remember that as a young acting student in New York in the 1970s, I and other starving students used to go to Bloomie's frequently to get spritzed with free perfume on the first floor and then to fill up on all those little food freebies they handed out in the cookware department.

I took a quick shower, put on jeans and a shirt, fought with the chaos in the closet until I located my raincoat, and took a cab uptown.

Igal was waiting for me at one of the high tables in the coffee shop.

I sat across from him on a high-back stool.

"All right," he said, practically gritting his teeth, "let's get on with it, shall we?"

"Top of the morning to you too, Igal."

"What? Oh, excuse me. Good afternoon, Miss Nestleton."

I looked at the tall, creamy café au lait before him on the table.

"Is the coffee good here?"

"Delicious. Here, take mine." He pushed the cup across to me. "If it will speed things up any."

"Thanks. Is there any sugar?"

I thought he was going to pick up the coffee and conk me one with it.

"As you know, Igal, you told me your wife was a photographer."

"She was."

"And that she made money from her hobby."

"She did."

"Did she have a darkroom in the house?"

"No. She sent her film out to a lab."

"What kind of professional help did you give her?"

"You know . . . hints about cropping, labs, prices, matting."

"What kind of photos did she take?"

"What kind? All kinds. Still lifes, portraits—"

"Cats?"

"I don't know. Maybe. I saw some. I saw some of people as well. And maybe even a few Martians."

I ignored his comment. I looked past our table. Next to us were seated two beautifully dressed South American women with a vast array of shopping bags.

One of their bags, I could see, held two intricately embroidered pillows. How I love expensive pillows.

At another table was an Asian couple with a child who was misbehaving. The father sat there eating placidly while the little boy shredded napkins and made lethal missiles from his tuna salad.

"Well?" Igal asked impatiently. "Is that all?"

"You're lying to me, aren't you, Igal?"

"About what?"

"About Wilma being a photographer."

"Oh, I see. The entertainment is about to begin, isn't it? You're going to start throwing around wild charges again."

"Why are you lying, Igal?" I snapped viciously, hoping it would throw him off.

But he snapped right back at me. "I told you the truth, you madwoman!" He stood up and started away from the table.

"Everyone else refutes you," I said quickly.

He stopped "Refutes what?"

"That Wilma had anything to do with photography. Nobody has ever even seen a camera in the office."

He sat back down, placed his hands on top of his head, and gave a low groan.

"Tell me something," he said after a minute. "If I go ahead and admit I killed her, will they deport me?"

"I'm not sure," I said honestly. "Why do you ask that?"

"Because, between those two idiot policemen and

your campaign of harassment, being an American isn't worth it. I'd rather give a false confession and get the hell out of this country."

Igal did something surprising then. He laughed. It was a laugh of resignation, but a laugh nonetheless.

"Listen, Miss Nestleton. I don't have to provide proof for my statements in this area."

"Why not?"

"Because you are the proof!"

"How so?"

"You were in her sitting room on the morning of the murder, weren't you? You saw her photographs."

"What are you talking about? Where were they?"

"Along the wall. Seven or eight shots. She never bragged about them, but they were on the wall for anybody to see. Mostly portraits, if I remember."

I was so astonished I was unable to speak. I remembered what was on the walls of the sitting room that morning. Prints of paintings of big cats—leopards and cheetahs and the like. They were rather awful. There had been no photographs of any kind.

"Suddenly you look sick, Miss Nestleton."

"Do I?" I said, feeling as if there were lead in my stomach.

Yes, I suppose I was sick.

For it was now clear to me that the murderer of Wilma Tedescu had removed her photographs from the sitting room and replaced them with those dumb jungle-cat paintings.

There was a grave look on Igal's face. "Are you sure you're—"

"Yes, Igal. It's okay."

"Good. I'll be running along then. They always sell out of my size early, you know."

Chapter 12

Nora was seated in the back booth at Pal Joey. She looked forlorn.

But once I was up close, I could tell she was a bit tipsy. I slid into the booth opposite her.

"What'll you have, honey?" she asked.

"Water."

"We don't serve water," she said, laughing. In front of her was what looked like a gin and tonic.

"What are you doing?" I asked, pointing to the legal pad and pen on the table in front of her. "That looks serious."

"I am plotting a change in the menu," she said in a conspiratorial voice.

"Why? I thought your customers loved the food."

"So what? What is a chef, anyway, if not an artist?

What do I care what my customers like? I want to give them something that will stretch their palates."

"So you're going to be a food pioneer—a kind of culinary trailblazer?"

"Damn right. Remember the Quilted Giraffe?"

"It was a bit too pricey for me, but I remember hearing of it. Is it still in business?"

"No. They closed down a few years ago. But what a run it had, Alice! It was really the first innovative restaurant in New York. It made the breakthrough. The dishes were so imaginative. The service was orchestrated. The presentation of the food was architectural. Ah yes, it was a joy."

She leaned back and smiled as if savoring memories. "They made the act of eating in a restaurant into performance art. And, I may add, they were the first to serve Blow Your Mind dishes."

"What's that?"

"Disharmonious dishes. Did you know that the restaurant critic from the *Times* trashed the Quilted Giraffe because they had a dish in which pickled herring in cream sauce was served with blueberries?"

"That is nauseating," I replied.

"Only at first sight. Because you are trained by habit not to put those foods together. Actually, it is quite delicious."

"And you're going to put dishes like that on your menu?"

"Yes . . . well, maybe. To be quite honest, I haven't been able to come up with too many yet."

She gestured to the bartender for another drink. It arrived quickly.

She doodled on the pad. Then her eyes lit up happily. "Wait! I think I have one. How about calf's brains sautéed in garlic butter, served with butter pecan ice cream?"

"That," I announced, "is the most sickening thing I have ever heard of in my life."

"Alice, you're a hopeless provincial."

"Agreed."

And then suddenly my friend burst into tears. I just stared dumbly at her.

Before I could think what to do, she recovered.

Nora held her hands up to show it was no matter. "I've been a bit crazy all day, Alice. I woke up this morning, looked at the ceiling, and realized the only thing I wanted to do was a simple song-and-dance routine. I wanted to perform again. Just once more. I want to belt out a song. Do you know that feeling, Alice? Do you know it?"

Poor Nora. I wanted to hug her.

"Anyway," she said, "I may not be doing too well, but you don't seem to be doing much better. You look all washed out."

"I just came from Bloomingdale's," I replied.

"Bad, huh?"

"I saw a ghost, Nora."

"Who? Anne Klein?"

"No. In the coffee shop. One ghost. Two dead women."

"Have a drink, Alice. You're not making any more sense than I was."

"On the morning of the murder, Nora, I was in the sitting room waiting for Wilma Tedescu."

"Yeah, I know that."

"Hung in the sitting room were paintings of big cats."

"Uh-huh. So?"

"I now know that they'd been hung only seconds before I entered. What really had hung there—photographs taken by Wilma—had been removed from the walls."

"That *is* weird."

I was weary and becoming a bit frightened. "I never came across anything like this. There was obviously a double murder, set ten years apart. And the murders become more baffling with every turn, because each piece of evidence, each clue, seems to shift in significa- tion and direction."

"Here's to bafflement!" Nora raised her glass and toasted. She drank the whole drink.

"You'd better calm down with that stuff, Nora."

She waved to the bartender. "Don't be silly," she chastised me. "Besides, I need all this to help you get rid of all this bafflement quickly. Aren't I your trusty sidekick? Don't I know what's going on?"

"I think I'd better get home. I have a lot of thinking to do."

"Well," she said testily, "if you don't want me to help you wrap up this case fast—go on home."

"Okay, Nora. Wrap it up."

"You're going about it the wrong way. You're not the old Alice Nestleton. Maybe Aaron getting difficult was too much for you. Oh, you sirens."

"What's the right way?"

"Forget about Wilma."

"Really?"

"Start with the other woman."

"Jane Doe?"

"Right. All you really have to do is find out who she was and the whole thing will come tumbling down. I mean, the whole thing will just fall into place. Like a good salad."

"Nora, she is called Jane Doe because no one has been able to find out who she was. Not even the combined talents of the NYPD."

"But Joseph Vise told you who she was. I heard him. The other night."

"What are you talking about? Vise told us nothing."

"Sure he did. He told you who she was. He said she was the wife of a dead psychiatrist."

"There are a lot of dead psychiatrists, Nora."

She shook her finger at me in a scolding manner.

"There are a lot fewer dead psychiatrists than dead dentists," she said.

It was, on the face of it, a nonsensical statement. But I did see the kernel of wisdom hidden in the husk of nonsense.

Oh yes, my friend had something.

"Do you have any quarters, Nora?"

She handed over a few and I rushed to the telephone and dialed Alison's number. Felix picked up the phone. Alison was out shopping, he said.

"It's you I want to talk to, Felix."

After all, he was a psychiatrist by training, though he no longer practiced and most of his work in that field I knew had been in constructing certification tests and procedures.

"Well, I'm here."

"Where do I find dead psychiatrists, Felix?"

"In the grave."

"I know that, dear. I mean information on them."

"What kind of information?"

"Names, for one. Places of residence and work, for another."

"Well, I guess you can call up the professional societies and ask them who died recently."

"I'm looking for psychiatrists who died between 1978 and 1984."

There was a pause.

"Did you hear me, Felix?"

"Yes. I'm thinking. Give me a minute."

I waited. I could hear him breathing.

"*JAMA,*" he finally said.

"What?"

"*JAMA. The Journal of the American Medical Association*. It's a magazine. It comes out weekly."

"And they print obituaries?"

"Religiously. Every issue."

"Where do I find it?"

"Any library, I guess."

"The public library?"

"On second thought, maybe not. You know the best place to go? The Cornell Medical School Library."

"Where is it?"

"Near New York Hospital. It's right smack on York Avenue. You can't miss it."

"Can anyone go in?"

"I think the only ones they keep out are the homeless."

"Which I'm not, Felix. Thanks to you."

"Don't worry, Alice. In a couple of years I may start charging you rent for the loft."

"Bless you, Felix. Say hello to Alison for me."

I hung up and returned to the booth. Nora was making notes on her pad.

"I need your help again, Nora."

"For what?"

"The Cornell Medical Library. It's on York Avenue. Can someone else work the kitchen for you now and maybe later?"

"I'm the boss here, Alice. I do what I like."

"Will you help me?"

"But what about my dish? I was planning the first experiment. Imagine the look on the faces of that couple from Roslyn, Long Island. They come in for the early-bird special to the Pal Joey Bistro they love. They order one of our signature dishes—excellent but mundane. What they get instead is a magnificent platter, artfully presented, of calf's brains with a scoop of the ice cream on each side of the plate. Is anything more important than this?"

"Yes. Dead psychiatrists."

Nora found that very funny. She leaned over and snarled, "Okay, babe. I'll meet you in the alley. Let me strap on some hardware first."

The library was filled with medical students who seemed to use their little carrels for sleeping as well as studying.

Nora and I were not asked for passes or cards or anything. The librarians, if that is what they were, were extremely accommodating. They showed us exactly where the back issues of *JAMA* could be found and then withdrew.

Nora whispered, "Maybe they called security. Maybe they think we're escapees from the closed ward at Payne Whitney."

But no security guards came. We found the relevant issues of *JAMA*—about three hundred of them—and then, pad and pencil in front of us, we began to search.

Felix, as usual, had been right.

Each issue contained an obituary page in the back.

Sometimes the section ran only one column, usually two columns, and occasionally there was an entire page full of the morbid tidings.

The obits were spartan.

Each one contained the name of the deceased; the type of medicine he or she practiced—psychiatry, obstetrics, etc.; where educated; date and cause of death; hospital or university affiliations; and names of survivors.

When we came upon a dead psychiatrist, we wrote the basic data on our pads.

"Why don't we just Xerox the page?" Nora asked.

It was another brilliant idea. The library, however, had coin-operated reproducing machines, so I had to go from deli to deli on York, begging for change of a dollar . . . and another dollar and another dollar.

We went through the issues in less than three hours, and we ended up with seventy-one sheets that contained the obituaries of eighty-two dead psychiatrists.

We strutted out of the library triumphantly.

"Now what?" Nora asked.

"Now Joseph Vise."

"You mean show him the list . . . jog his memory?"

"Exactly."

"Let's go."

"Wait. There's a problem."

"What problem?"

"I don't think Joseph Vise will be happy to see us.

I distinctly remember that he no longer loves his cat-sitters."

"Oh! He's an old dear, Alice. He was just a bit out of sorts that you cornered him, that he had to reveal an old affair he didn't want to reveal. Actually, I think he wasn't between wives like he said. I think he was still married at the time to one wife or another and he's old-fashioned enough to be ashamed of adultery."

"What a quaint word," I noted.

"What word?"

"Adultery."

We both laughed. Then Nora's face lit up.

"I have an idea. It's utterly shameless, but I think it will do the trick. Joseph Vise just adores marzipan. I remember a long conversation we once had about marzipan at the Bistro. We were both just the slightest bit drunk. Anyway, he told me that if he were about to be executed, marzipan would be his choice for a last meal."

"Then let's get some. Where should we go?"

"I know just the place. He told me about a store that specializes in it. It's somewhere on East Eighty-sixth Street."

'Do you remember the name of the store?"

"No."

We took a cab up York Avenue to Eighty-sixth. Then Nora walked west on Eighty-sixth on the north side of the street and I took the south side.

I found the place quickly; the spotless little shop

between Second and Third avenues was long on charm and short on space. No need for Christmas decorations there; it was already decked out like a little enchanted cottage. The windows were filled with hundreds of tiny animals—pigs, cows, cats—all made of marzipan. And the salespeople—a father and daughter—were like the kindly burghers in a German fairy tale.

"A caloric wonderland," Nora said as we entered.

The young woman with blond braids was busy behind the glass counter. A tiger-striped cat lounged on top of the front radiator. I almost expected him to talk to us.

We studied the wares carefully.

"Let's not overdo it," Nora suggested.

"By all means, no," I said in agreement.

But we did overdo it.

I purchased a half pound of small chocolate-covered marzipan squares. Then three plain logs. Then two dancing piggies. Then a donkey with raspberry jelly ears.

And Nora, caught up in the frenzy, bought a little marzipan piano with milk chocolate keys.

Then we took a cab downtown to Vise's building. We had decided not to call first, just to show up in the lobby and announce ourselves to the doorman as more or less "expected."

Joseph Vise kept us waiting downstairs an inordinately long time and I began to get nervous. But then the summons came, and when we stepped out of the elevator he was waiting for us in a welcoming manner at his door.

The old actor was wearing a tan cashmere jacket with dark blue trousers.

Once inside, Nora and I immediately began to lay the candy out on the coffee table. Vise rocked back and forth on his heels. He looked as if he were trying to restrain himself. Yes, I thought, this man has a severe marzipan problem. And at his age!

When the sweet stuff was all laid out, he asked, "May I?"

At my nod, he reached down and plucked a single chocolate-covered marzipan square from the procession.

Joe performed an elaborate piece of stage business then. He held the item up for the audience to see, admiring its shape and balance, then slowly slid it through the puckered portals of his lips, then chewed thoughtfully, his entire face shining with pleasure at each bite.

It was an astonishing performance. And when he had finally swallowed it all, Nora and I applauded.

"Thank you, thank you," Joseph Vise said with a bow. Then he straightened up. "Why do I have the strange feeling that I've just been bribed?"

"You damn well have," Nora said.

That was my cue. I pulled out the sheets and handed them to him.

"What are these?"

"Xeroxed obituaries of dead psychiatrists from the *Journal of the American Medical Association*."

"They used to say that Charles Laughton could fill a theater just reading a telephone book. Is this a theatrical offer, Alice? You want me to read obits in a one-man show?"

"No. I want you to look through them and see if any name rings a bell."

"In my head?"

"Exactly."

"A church bell or a doorbell?"

"Any kind."

"Ah. This is about the poor woman in the beach photo. The widow woman."

"Yes."

He grinned broadly and picked up one of the dancing pigs.

"Oh, I tell you. Two things I can never get my fill of: marzipan and you beautiful women. You'll kill me yet."

He polished off the piggy. Then he extricated his glasses from their case, put them on, and began to read.

I looked at Nora. She crossed her fingers. Roberta strolled in to check me out. She sniffed at the goodies on the coffee table, didn't find them interesting at all, and strolled away.

"Why don't you sit down, Joe," I suggested.

"Excellent idea," he replied. We vacated the sofa in front of the marzipan for him.

The apartment became very quiet except for the slight rustle when he turned a page.

My neck was beginning to get stiff. Nora lost herself in one of her silent reveries. Was it calf's brains again?

Joe reached for another candy. I was so tense I literally jumped. He picked up on my tenseness and smiled. He ate the candy, took off his glasses, rubbed his eyes, replaced the spectacles, and went back to the obituaries.

I walked to the window and stared down on lovely Washington Square Park.

Then Nora said, "I think I'm going to diminish the bribe." She picked up a piece of marzipan.

Joseph Vise said, "Tintinnabulation."

"What?" Nora asked, thinking that Joseph was objecting to the theft.

But I burst out: "The tintinnabulation of the bells, bells, bells. Edgar Allan Poe!"

"Exactly," Joseph said.

"The bells are ringing!" I shouted and ran to the sofa.

Joseph tapped the paper.

"This one sounds familiar," he said.

The name was James Parrish. He lived and worked in New Haven, Connecticut. He had died of a massive cerebral stroke at the age of sixty-two on June 11, 1981. He had left a wife named Ann.

I picked up the paper and kissed Joseph.

Then I walked into one of the bedrooms and sat down on the bed by the phone.

I had to compose myself. I had to think clearly. The trail had suddenly gotten hot . . . scorching in fact . . . and I needed all the help I could get.

I picked up the phone, then put it back down. No. It would be best to make the calls from my loft. I was only a twenty-minute walk from home.

I went back into the living room. Nora and Joseph were discussing the fine points of the marzipan piano.

"I have to go," I announced. Then added: "Nora, why don't you stay for a while and help Joe destroy the evidence."

"I shall, gladly," she announced.

"Thank you, Joseph," I said.

Then I rushed home. Bushy and Pancho did not appreciate my manic state. I fed them. Then called Felix. He and Alison were in the midst of supper.

"What are you eating?"

"Lamb."

"Remember the Blake poem about lambs?"

"No."

"Neither do I, Felix. But I need your help again. I found the dead psychiatrist where you said I'd find him."

"Oh really?"

"Yes. And now I need to know a little more about him. Like what kind of psychiatry he practiced."

"Why?"

"Will it be difficult to find that out, Felix?" I asked, ignoring his question completely.

"The American Psychiatric Association puts out a biographical directory every few years. I have all of them upstairs, going back to the 1950s. Just give me his name and when he died."

I gave him the information, apologized for being a pest, thanked him again, sent my love to my niece, and hung up.

Then I began to prepare myself mentally for the next call—the important call. To Aaron Stoner.

It was growing dark outside. The day had been long, but the rewards great. My fingers trembled when I dialed. There was no answer. I left a message on the machine to call me immediately.

He called back in twenty minutes. He had a funny catch in his voice. It was obvious to me that he thought I was calling to capitulate, to profess my undying and exclusive love for him, to swear that I had rid myself of all obsessions but him.

I disabused him of that immediately. I fairly shouted into the phone: "I know who your Jane Doe is."

There was silence.

Then I heard him flipping the pages of the notebook.

He said in a clipped, professional voice: "Go ahead."

I read the obituary. I told him it had jogged Joseph Vise's memory.

Aaron spoke the name once: "Ann Parrish."

He gave a little laugh, a strange little laugh, and then he said, "I'll get back to you tomorrow," and hung up.

When I opened my eyes the first thing I saw was Bushy sniffing and pacing and prancing over near the cabinet where I keep the cat food. He had probably been trying to wake me for hours.

It was nearly 10 A.M.! I never sleep that late.

But what a wonderful sleep it had been—deep and untroubled—the way sleep was meant to be.

Outside, the clouds had all rolled away. I lay there and watched the crystalline morning sun flooding the loft.

Yuck. The apartment was a mess. Dust everywhere.

After I had coffee and fed the starving beasts, I started to clean the loft, humming as I worked. There was no shortage of work to do. Not least was the ocean of laundry that had piled up since the washing machine went on the blink last month. I kept meaning to either have it repaired or take everything to the laundry on Hudson Street. Somehow I just hadn't gotten around to it.

I plucked out of the pantry the pathetic broken straw broom that I had purchased many years ago at the Lighthouse Shop of Blind Handicrafts.

The cats were gloating as I began to sweep. They hated my vacuum cleaner above all else in the world, and had been relieved when it broke down a few weeks ago.

Then I began the mopping. Not my favorite thing in the world. But then again, what household task was? I was never much good at those domestic chores, and the people who could iron baby clothes, re-spackle the shower stall, and whip up a batch of popovers at the same time had my admiration. Not my envy, but my admiration.

Halfway through the mopping I felt a twinge of pain in my back and straightened up.

I caught a glimpse of myself in the full-length mirror Tony Basillio had bought for me as a housewarming present. It was now simply standing against a wall, buttressed from falling by three cinder blocks also provided by Tony.

The image in the mirror astonished me.

That was *me*?

No, it couldn't be. The woman in the mirror was wearing a cheap cotton dress over a leotard and wielding a mop.

That woman wasn't long, leggy Alice, the actress. She was a household drudge. She was middle-aged. She was putting on weight. Her face looked drawn and a bit lined. And her famous golden hair was in dire need of a touch-up.

Where had all the flowers gone?

The floor was only half done and I was expecting a couple of important calls, but right then I thought it best to get out of the house for a while.

I dropped the mop, grabbed the laundry bags, and walked out of the loft.

Once on the street I felt better, much better. It was a brisk, beautiful morning. I headed for the Laundromat just three blocks away, run by an extended family of Vietnamese immigrants.

The store contained a long double row of washers and dryers for those who wished to do their laundry themselves.

For the rich and lazy, like myself, there was a counter and scale where the bundles were dropped off to be done by the nephews, of which there were many.

There was a line for the rich and lazy that morning, so I took my place on it and waited.

Not twenty feet from the line, a young woman sat in front of a washing machine. At her feet was a wicker basket containing a huge box of detergent.

She was rather beautiful, rather severe. Her long brown hair was pinned atop her head with a huge barrette. She wore a tattered flannel shirt tied at the waist, scruffy jeans, and dirty red Converse sneakers. No makeup at all.

She was completely engrossed in the paperback she was reading. On top of her head perched a pair of dark glasses.

Without doubt she was an actress. I felt a surge of affection and nostalgia and then a sharp twinge of sadness. She was me, twenty years ago.

I shifted my position on the line to get a glimpse of the book's title.

Oh my! It was William Redfield's *Letters from an Actor*. A wonderful insider's book about the staging of Gielgud's *Hamlet* on Broadway with Richard Burton in the title role. A delicious mélange of theater gossip and wisdom swirling around the 1964 production, done in street clothes and featuring, in addition to Burton (and Elizabeth Taylor waiting for him after each performance), Alfred Drake, Hume Cronyn, Eileen Herlie, George Voskovec, to name just a few. The author, Redfield, played Guildenstern.

I was a very young woman in Minnesota when I read that book, and it hit me like the King James Bible hits a born-again sinner.

Sinner. Actress. Laundry.

I had begun to play a strange kind of word-association game with myself. What was that all about?

Then I remembered my agent's call. That's right! I was—perhaps—going to play a frontier laundress in a Canadian television series about the French and Indian War.

Well, here was my chance to start preparing for the part. Why didn't I just do this mass of dirty clothes myself? Get into the suds and the rinsing and the—

My turn at the scale came before the fantasy could be implemented. And the sound of the bag plopping down on the scale brought me back to reality.

"Wash and fold?" asked the girl at the counter.

"Yes," I said. "Wash and fold."

I took the ticket and walked out.

The moment I arrived back in the loft, I saw the blinking red light of the telephone answering machine.

I rushed over and pressed the PLAY button.

The first call was from Felix.

"Alice, it's Felix. Your dead psychiatrist, James Parrish, specialized in childhood disorders with emphasis on schizophrenia. Come to dinner next Thursday—okay? I'm making sushi. See you soon."

Well, I thought, at least Parrish wasn't a cat therapist.

The second message was from Aaron Stoner. It was monotone, as if he were reading from a notebook. He didn't even bother to identify himself.

"You were right. My Jane Doe is Ann Parrish. She vanished from New Haven ten years ago. Prior to disappearing she requested police protection from New Haven PD. Request was denied.

"Further inquiry yielded the following: In 1982 a woman named Wilma Leland, living in Old Saybrook, renewed an expired Connecticut driver's license.

"Records also show that the same Wilma Leland gave birth to a daughter, Angela, in the U.S. Naval Hospital in New London, Connecticut, in 1974.

"Information on Leland/Tedescu given to Detectives Rush and Morrow. Your name not mentioned."

I felt weak in the knees.

A daughter?

So Wilma had a child—a daughter.

Where did she come from? Where was she now? Why hadn't anyone mentioned her?

The possibilities started bursting out all over, an endless list of them.

What if Rita Falco was really this daughter—Angela?

What if Raymond Dunn was Angela's father?

Or Wyatt Tanner?

What did this daughter have to do with Ann Parrish?

I played the tape twice more to make sure I had heard it correctly. I had. No doubt about it. The bottle was open and the genie had slipped out.

Chapter 13

"Again?!"

Igal's voice was incredulous.

"Yes. Again," I said. "I need to see you again."

There was a bitter laugh at the other end of the line.

"Are you of Rumanian descent?" he asked.

"Of course not."

"I was beginning to get the feeling that you were. That your people really were born in the Carpathian Mountains. That's in Transylvania."

"You mean I'm really a vampire."

"It's possible," he said.

"You may have something there, Igal," I agreed. "I do seem to always have my fangs buried in your neck, don't I? Draining you dry. Extracting all your secrets."

"And my sanity," he added. "Well, dear Alice, what

shall we do today? Best friends that we are, why don't we go shopping again? You can interrogate me as we go."

"Again?" It was my turn to be incredulous.

"Oh yes," he said. "You know me—always looking for a bargain."

We didn't go back to Bloomingdale's. Igal said there was a men's clothing store at Seventeenth and Park Avenue South that he wanted to check out.

Igal was already there when I arrived, picking over the ties on the sale rack just inside the entrance. As usual, he cut a lithe and handsome figure.

It was the quietest shop I had ever been in. Not a single concession to the Christmas frenzy; no tree, no Santas, no bells, no reindeers. And no Christmas rush at all. The handful of well-dressed customers were examining the merchandise or filing into the dressing rooms or discreetly handing over their plastic at the register without making a sound.

I followed Igal silently from counter to counter.

"I have a gift certificate. I am looking for a winter sweater," he announced.

"A nice red one with reindeer?"

"Again you are confusing me with someone else, Miss Nestleton. I am Rumanian, not Scandinavian."

"The reindeer has become universal, Igal. It's even in Brooklyn," I counseled him.

"What do you think of this one?" he asked. He was

holding a lush gray sweater against his chest. It had a kind of Aztec motif across the top.

"Is what I think important to you?"

He gave me a strange look. Like he craved some kind of compassion. Like he feared me. Like my person unsettled him. I realized that his look explained why I always wanted to meet him face-to-face rather than speak on the phone. He *was* afraid of me in some sense. And he did crave my approval. Shame on you, Alice, I thought. Does power over another person now titillate you?

"The interrogation, as you call it, is starting right now," I announced.

He checked the price tag again and folded the sweater fastidiously.

"Good," he said.

"It's going to be a very short interrogation, Igal. Only one question."

"That's even better."

"Where is Angela?"

He looked blankly at me. "Who?"

"Angela."

"I don't think I know any Angelas. I am acquainted with an Annette and an Anita, and even an Anastasia. But no Angelas."

"All I need is one Angela, Igal. And you certainly do know her."

"I told you, I don't."

"You're saying you don't know Wilma's daughter, Angela? Never even heard of her? Hard to believe."

"What are you talking about? What daughter?"

"Wilma Leland had a daughter, born some twenty-two years ago in a New London hospital. And named Angela."

He didn't reply.

"Do you mean to tell me that you were married to a woman for five years . . . that she shared the same house with you . . . and she never once mentioned her child?"

He looked shaken. "I never knew, I tell you."

I was becoming angry.

"That is unbelievable. That she wouldn't even mention the name Angela."

A salesman sidled over, obviously worried by the rising tone of my voice.

"Can I be of any help?"

"None at all," I replied.

Abandoning the sweater, Igal walked quickly out of the store. I followed him.

"What about a photo of her?" I yelled after him. "You told me she was a photographer. Surely the loving mother would have a photo of her child."

"Leave me alone," he called back.

I shut up. This was getting me nowhere at all. The genie was being forced back into the bottle. I put my hands on the glass window of the store. It calmed me.

I knew that if I could find Angela—if I could even

find a picture of her—a gruesome double murder would unravel.

I looked at Igal. He was staring down at his polished shoes. There was no doubt in my mind that only he could lead me to Angela.

The police, of course, still believed that Igal had murdered his wife. But I no longer believed that. And he surely didn't murder Ann Parrish. Poor Igal. He wasn't a sharpie who was going to parlay ownership of a little downtown café into a restaurant empire. He wasn't a shark. He was the kind of European whom this country, and this city, sooner or later eats up and spits out.

But I needed him.

"Tell me, Igal, did Wilma ever mention the name Ann Parrish?"

"No. Not Ann. Not Angela. I've never heard those names. I swear it."

When he got agitated his impeccable English seemed to break apart and you could hear the foreign accent.

"We found a photograph of Ann Parrish that was probably taken by Wilma."

"I'm sure she took pictures of a lot of people."

"Do you think a photo of her daughter exists?"

"I suppose so. *If* she had a daughter, I suppose so." He looked to be on the verge of tears. "Imagine that . . . her child . . . I don't understand."

I put my hand on his arm.

"Listen to me, Igal. Unless I find Wilma's murderer, the police are going to hound you until the day you die. I can get them off your back if you help me. Do you understand? I mean really help me."

"How am I supposed to do that? I don't even understand half the things you say to me."

"Let me be simple. Why do you think Wilma was so secretive about her photography when she was so open and even proud of her cat practice?"

"I don't know."

"Is this kind of secrecy common among photographers?"

"Not among hobbyists. But with art photographers or fashion photographers—yes, it does happen. I never knew why. They start to act like prima donnas. Like *artistes*."

"How would you go about looking for a photo of Angela Leland?"

"Shot by Wilma?"

"Yes."

"I don't know. Maybe she destroyed all her photos except for the ones she hung in her waiting room."

"They were removed by the murderer."

He was startled. "Why would he do that? They were nothing special, if I recall."

"I haven't the slightest idea, Igal. Let's get back to the real problem."

"Which is?"

"Where do I find a photo of Angela, if it exists?"

He was silent for a long time, shifting his body from side to side ever so slightly.

"Maybe there's a negative," he finally said.

"Where?"

"I don't know. Maybe in the house somewhere. I told you what kind of person Wilma was. She might have hidden it under a floorboard, the way she hid money. Or maybe it's in a processing lab somewhere."

"A lab?"

"Yes, Wilma didn't take her film to the local pharmacy or one of those two-hour jokes. She used a lab like the pros use. You send film to them. They give you back the contact sheets. You select the ones you want and give them instructions on enlarging, cropping, brushing. The lab holds on to the negatives until it's all finished. And sometimes they hold on to material for a long time."

I was beginning to tingle. Igal was making very good sense.

"Do you know which one she might have used?"

"Any one of several."

"Where are they?"

"Well, three of the better ones are in the Twenties, around Broadway."

"That's five minutes away," I said.

"So?"

"Listen, Igal. We just walk into each lab. You tell them the truth: your wife died. You know she sent in several rolls of film to get processed a few days before she died. You want them back. They're precious to you now. As a memento of her. You want whatever of hers they have."

He seemed a bit frightened at the prospect.

"It's important, Igal. It's crucial. The only way you'll ever be cleared, in my opinion, is to find this Angela or a likeness of her. It's the stumbling block. Don't you get it? It has to be. I know it is. From the very beginning I kept grasping at straws. This is no straw, however. This has to be the linchpin."

"What is a linchpin?"

"Later," I said. "I'll tell you later."

We walked uptown. The first photo lab we entered was on Twentieth Street between Broadway and Fifth; a cavernous place with action ski posters papering the walls.

The tall red-haired man behind the counter with a University of Miami sweatshirt listened to Igal's script.

Then he said, "The name doesn't ring a bell. But I'll check."

The glass-covered counter between us was cool to the touch.

"Did you ever use this place?" I asked Igal after the counterman had vanished into the back.

"A couple of times. Years ago. Now I do everything myself. I have a small photographic studio on Stanton Street. It's a closet."

The gentleman with the University of Miami shirt returned in about five minutes.

He turned his hands over in a shrug. "Nothing," he said.

"Well, thank you anyway," Igal replied. We headed out the door.

"I am sorry about your wife," the counterman called out.

We both turned back to acknowledge the kindly condolences from a stranger.

But what we saw on the redhead's face was a leer.

The next place was a block uptown and a block west.

This lab was smaller and cluttered. A bell rang when we entered, and a heavyset woman in a denim dress came out of the back. She had a pencil behind one ear.

As we approached the counter she held up her hands in mock horror and said, "Don't tell me. Let me guess. Lawyers? Cops? Tax people?"

"None of the above," I replied.

"Okay. How may I help you?"

Igal gave his little speech.

When he was finished the woman searched about on the cluttered counter until she found a pad. Then she pulled the pencil from behind her ear, gave it to Igal, and said, "Write the name."

Igal wrote in a labored print: Wilma Tedescu.

I took the pad away from him, scratched it out, and wrote Wilma Leland Tedescu.

The woman took the slip and walked along the

counter to one of those elaborate little computers, the kind one sees in restaurant bars, with a receipt printer and a cash register attached.

We followed her down the counter.

She punched the name in. She frowned. She punched some more. She tried several different combinations. Then she handed the slip back to Igal.

"Your wife is not one of our customers," she said. "Otherwise, she would be in our computer."

As we left she suggested, "Why don't you try Pearl Labs. They're on Nineteenth Street."

"Yes. I know about them," Igal replied.

Pearl Labs was on the second floor of a very dingy building. The young counterman, with a bowl haircut, was seated on a high stool reading a paperback British mystery. The book looked as if it had been rained on in an outdoor stall of a secondhand bookstore. The title was something like *The Derelict Garden Murders*.

When he saw us he didn't get up. He just stared.

Igal gave the speech.

The young man grimaced.

Then he said, "Do you think I just fell off the back of the cabbage truck? If in fact your wife was one of our customers, do you think I would just release the materials to you? What about identification? How do I know the two of you aren't blackmailers or something? How do I know . . ." He stopped in the middle of his sentence.

"Actually," Igal twitted him, "you are right to be

suspicious. I am an agent from the Rumanian Secret Police."

I joined in the fun. "And I am his assistant from Transylvania. Do you know what that means?" I laid on the Bela Lugosi accent.

The young man pulled his turtleneck down to expose his neck. Then he went back to his mystery, ignoring us.

Igal tapped on the counter with his ring.

"Are you going to help us?" he asked angrily.

"No ticket, no shirt," the young man replied in an infuriatingly sardonic voice.

Igal stalked out. I followed him.

We went into the Old Town Bar, on Eighteenth Street, and took a booth. Igal ordered a Mexican liqueur and I ordered a bottle of ale.

"This is not working," Igal said.

"You have a point," I said.

We drank in glum silence for about five minutes.

And then, suddenly, Igal burst out laughing.

"What's so funny?" I asked.

"I was thinking how strange people in New York are."

"You mean the suspicion?"

"Yes. That woman thought we might be cops. And the young man in the last lab was totally crazy."

I started to laugh. "At least," I said, "he knew how people entertain themselves in Transylvania."

We had finished our drinks but neither of us moved.

The waitress asked us if we wanted anything else. When we said we didn't, she took a pencil out of her hair and wrote the check out by the booth, leaving it on the table.

"My grandmother used to do it like that," I noted.

"Like what?"

"The pencil stuck in the hair. When we went into town to shop, she put her list on her sleeve with a safety pin and pushed a pencil into her hair."

The memory, for some reason, agitated me. I pressed my back against the booth to calm down. Igal stared moodily at the check.

No. I realized it wasn't the memory that had disturbed me. It was the pencil. In my grandmother's hair. Like the waitress.

No. It was the pencil behind the ear of the stout woman with the denim dress in the photo lab.

No. It wasn't the pencil. My imagination seemed to be racing.

It was the salutation. The one Igal had commented on. But Igal had left two thirds of it out. The woman had jokingly asked if we were cops, lawyers, or tax people.

Tax people? Why that?

What a strange thing to say, even as a joke.

I closed my eyes and tried to visualize the episode, minutely.

There was the cluttered counter. There was the

computer she had run the name check on . . . the one with the receipt printer.

There was the little pad she had given to Igal to write his wife's name on.

What else was on the counter?

I had seen some technical manuals; what looked like a receipt book; and a lot of glossy price sheets for blowups, silk-screening, and other developing processes. I couldn't remember anything else. I hadn't been looking carefully.

Only that receipt had been a little out of place.

It was an old-fashioned one—that I could tell. The kind one used to find in meat markets or hardware stores.

"Tell me, Igal, how do photo lab customers pay?"

"What do you mean?"

"Cash or check, for example."

"Check mostly. You bring your film in. They give you a receipt. When it's ready you pick it up and pay. A lot of them deliver COD and you pay the messenger. And a lot of customers are just billed monthly."

"So cash is very rare?"

"Only pros use these kinds of labs. They're in business. They pay their bills once a month. They're often late but they never pay cash."

I sat up so quickly I frightened Igal and he knocked the empty ale bottle over. A man at the bar stared at us, as if he were about to witness a juicy and violent lovers' quarrel.

It was suddenly obvious to me what was going on in that lab. Nothing uncommon.

There was a two-tier receipt system.

For regular customers there were the computer receipts. The formal system. Legitimate. All income reported and all taxes paid.

But for the rare cash customer there was the other system. The old-fashioned receipt book. The customer gets a receipt. The lab pockets the cash and never reports it.

That didn't mean anything, except that if Wilma had used the lab and paid cash, the woman in the lab wouldn't have told us. And Wilma surely wouldn't be on her computer.

Was there a chance that Wilma had used that lab and paid cash? I didn't know.

"Why are you making a face?" Igal asked.

"I'm thinking."

"You look like the fox that swallowed the canary."

I smiled at Igal's mangling of the metaphor.

"Let's just say that we're not dead yet, Igal."

"Do you want to know something really odd?" he said.

"What?"

"Actually, it's more than odd. It's insane, I guess. But I think I like you. It must be that syndrome they talk about. Like falling in love with the person who kidnaps you—identifying with your oppressor."

"A backhanded compliment if ever there was one," I said. "But I'll accept it anyway, Igal. Thanks."

I gathered my things and slid out of the booth.

"Where are you going?"

"You know the saying, 'Money talks'?"

"No."

"Well, it does. I'm going to the bank," I said.

I pressed BALANCE INQUIRY on the ATM machine and waited.

Four hundred dollars of my cat-sitting fee from Joseph Vise was still in the account.

I punched out $380 and got the cash. Then I walked into the bank proper, Igal following me like a shadow, and got three hundred dollar bills in return for the twenties I had gotten from the ATM. I put the three bills in a bank deposit envelope and put it in my purse.

"Now, Igal," I said, "let's return to the lady with the pencil behind her ear."

Off we went. She was with a customer when we entered. We waited at one end of the counter. When the customer left she didn't come over to us. So we walked over to her.

"Forget something?" she asked.

"Yes," I said. "We forgot to be generous."

I extracted the envelope from my purse and laid it on the counter. Then I opened the envelope flap and slid the bills halfway out.

The woman stared at the money.

"I don't know if we're talking about the same person," she said, "but if she's dead, I'm sorry."

"What did she look like?" I pressed.

"Big. Amazonian."

An excited Igal interrupted with a detailed but condensed description.

"Yes. That's her!" the woman said. She picked the bills out of the envelope, folded them, and placed the loot in a pocket of her denim dress.

I suddenly wished Tony Basillio was with me. He would have appreciated the whole sleazy transaction.

"She used to come in here every few months. She never gave me a name. She always paid cash."

"Did she pick up after it was done?" I asked.

"She never picked up a finished job. That was one of the strange things. When she paid up front, she gave us just a P.O. box. We sent the contact sheets there. Then she would come in with instructions, pay whatever else was required in cash, and give us another P.O. box to mail to."

"What kind of stuff was she bringing in?"

"That was even stranger."

"How so?"

"Did you ever see those life-size cardboard cutouts of presidents in front of novelty stores? They take a picture of you next to the cutout so it looks like you're shaking hands with George Bush or Bill Clinton."

"They still have them on Broadway."

"Well, that's essentially what she did. With a twist. She had these photos of men. Older men for the most part. And she had photos of herself. She spliced the two together and shot the combined photo to make it appear real. She told me she was making funny birthday cards for friends."

"Does this make sense to you, Igal?" I asked.

"No! I don't understand."

"What was funny about them?" I asked her.

"In the photos, she was naked and draped all over the men. They, the men, are wearing clothes. It was a kind of tender, soft-core pornography. Kind of innocent."

"Essentially, she was faking photographs," I said.

"I guess you can call it that."

"Did she ever tell you who the men were?"

"Not their names. She just said they were friends."

"What kinds of cards did she claim they were?"

"I told you. Birthday cards."

"Do you have any of her materials? Negatives? Contact sheets? Discarded prints? Anything?"

"No."

"What about the receipts? In the cash receipt book. Didn't you even keep a copy for yourself?"

"No."

My question made her uncomfortable. She looked away. She shook her head.

Igal whispered in my ear: "Wilma never sent a birthday card in her life."

"I don't know why. But the minute you people walked in I had the feeling that you were connected to her," she said musingly.

"Why? Because we pay cash you don't have to report?" I retorted.

She flushed.

Igal whispered again: "None of this makes any sense. What does it mean? What does it have to do with her daughter? If there is a daughter."

"I don't know yet, Igal."

But I did know one thing it meant. I was going back to Wilma Leland Tedescu's brownstone as fast as I could get access.

That was for sure.

Chapter 14

"Did you find anything the first time you were here?" Detective Rush asked.

"No," I replied. Of course, I had found quite a bit. Particularly the bogus appointment book.

"And that's what you'll find this time. We took the whole house apart and put it together again." Rush waited for me to comment. I didn't say anything. I could see him evaluating me . . . trying to figure out my relationship with Aaron Stoner . . . maybe trying to figure out the rumors about me. After all, I had consulted once with the NYPD. But it was several years ago and the only thing that had emerged from all that work was my ridiculous nickname—Cat Woman.

Then he gave up figuring and said, "Just slam the door on the way out. Believe it or not, the block association is taking care of janitorial services until the estate gets sorted out. The trouble is, Wilma Leland Tedescu seemed to exist alone . . . right . . . except for a murderous husband and some psychotic cat patients scattered throughout the city."

Oh, this Detective Rush is slick, I thought. He has switched gears and is now playing the naïf in order to pump me. To get me talking about the case.

Keep quiet, Alice, I counseled myself. And I did. He slammed the door on the way out. I wondered for a moment what kind of conversations Aaron Stoner was having with Rush and Morrow. Then I got to work.

This time I opened every door and drawer in every room of the house. I kicked at the floor and radiators to locate hidden chambers. I peered under beds and chests and bookcases.

What I was looking for was simple. Something photographic. Anything. Albums. Cameras. Negatives. Anything.

As I searched I kept pushing back a dread that one of the old men the woman in the lab had spoken about was Joseph Vise.

After all, Joe was the only person who knew both Ann and Wilma. Both had been murdered. Probably by the same person. Joe was suspect. He had to be. But I didn't want him to be a murderer. I wanted him to die happy, in his own bed, beloved by audiences.

Then I reached the waiting room and stared with distaste at the big-cat prints.

Now that I knew they had been put there by the murderer, I could view them with more objectivity. It was obvious the changeover had been done quickly and sloppily. The various prints did not perfectly fit the various frames that had held the photographs. But it did show that Wilma's murder had been premeditated. No one can find prints of wildlife art just hanging around. They were brought to the brownstone. It was planned substitution.

I walked into the office and sat on the dead woman's chair. I began to shiver, and I found myself touching my neck right behind each ear to make sure no bullet holes were there.

How nice it would have been if I could have seen Wilma Tedescu work, just once, treating a distraught feline with her tops and spinning toys.

I closed my eyes and tried to re-create the sounds of that terrible morning—Wilma's voice on the machine fooling me into thinking that it was her real voice.

But all my memory could retrieve was a dull hum and the trickle of blood from the ear and the little apron.

I opened my eyes and tried to think of a place that I had not searched in my rather desperate sweeps. Obviously, I was not a scientific researcher . . . if there was such a science.

But I had been thorough. I had been through everything in my fashion—from the kitchen to the hall closets to the radiators in all the rooms. I had peered, pulled, knocked, kicked.

Wilma was too smart for me. When she hid something it stayed hidden. The problem was, no one had the slightest idea what she was hiding, or why.

I tried to reason.

Where in my loft would I hide a photograph I didn't want anyone to see?

The steam pipe? No.

The loose tiles in the bathtub? No.

In the fabric of a chair? No.

Inside a light fixture? Maybe. But probably not, because of the danger of fire.

Then it came to me.

In the kitty litter pan, of course. No doubt about it.

But there was no kitty litter in Wilma's house. She didn't have any cats—she just treated them.

And treated them . . . and treated them . . . I whispered to myself . . . the neurotic, the psychotic, and the catatonic. The hiders and seekers. All the whacked-out cattys. . . .

I felt giddy. I knew! Oh yes. I knew.

I dashed to the cabinets and pulled all the drawers open. Then I scooped Wilma's therapeutic toys out wherever I found them—the spinning tops and the rest.

Grasping a large red, white, and blue top, I knocked it against the side of the desk as if it were a walnut.

The parts separated. Almost miraculously.

And into my hand fell a tiny scroll.

190 *Lydia Adamson*

I unrolled it. It was one horizontal strip cut from a contact sheet of photos. About twenty prints.

I stared at them in wonder. The woman in the lab had not lied.

Each one showed a disrobed Wilma leaning over or caressing an older man. It was almost impossible to tell they had been spliced together . . . that they were fake.

Joseph Vise, thankfully, was not one of the men.

I searched the other tops and found three more scrolls.

Nothing of the mythical Angela. Nor of Vise.

I laid them all out on the desk.

What had Wilma been doing?

One thing was clear. They weren't the gentle funny birthday cards the woman in the lab had claimed.

There was something menacing and ugly about all of them. I didn't know what they signified except that somehow, in some way, I was staring at the heart of the matter.

There was a fight going on behind the closed door of Nora's office at the back of the Pal Joey Bistro.

I decided to wait quietly outside the door until the smoke settled.

A minute later two burly men rushed out, yelling back at Nora that she was a liar and an idiot. What Nora yelled at them I cannot even reproduce.

She was seated, fuming, behind her desk.

"And where the hell have you been hiding yourself?" she demanded.

I didn't get a chance to answer. She flung a book at the wall savagely. "Did you see those two crooks, Alice? Can you believe them! I buy meat from them."

"What was the fight about?"

"Are you deaf, Alice? I just told you. They're crooks. And why don't you answer my question? Where the hell have you been?"

"Hither and thither," I replied, and then cleared a small space on her incredibly messy desk and laid out the contact-sheet strips.

"What is this?"

"Look, Nora."

Her eyes widened. "I know you've been alienating all your men friends lately, but has it come to this? Are things really this bad? Erotica?"

"The naked woman is Wilma Tedescu."

"And the men?"

"I haven't the slightest idea. They're fake photos, Nora. Two spliced together. It was poor Wilma's hobby."

"I thought her hobby was feline Freudianism."

"That was her business. This, as I said, was her hobby, though it must have been profit-making as well."

"So what are you going to do with them?"

"I think I'm going to exhibit them."

"This junk? You must be kidding."

"I'm quite serious."

"Well, I think you should spend your time getting back with Aaron Stoner. He looks like he's hurting."

"Everybody's hurting, Nora."

"Ain't it the truth? You need any more help, Alice? I have the feeling that you're up to something tricky."

"I need some money."

"How much?"

"About fourteen hundred dollars."

"Why not? Better you than the meat brothers."

It was a dingy store on Sullivan Street just north of Canal Street.

Mr. Golub opened the door as if it might fall off its hinges. He walked in. I followed, very gingerly. Both of us were searching for a light in the dim, narrow room. We found one on the wall and it activated a pathetic bare bulb in a very high lighting fixture.

"It's been empty for about three months," Mr. Golub claimed. "There used to be a handbag store here."

I walked up and down the narrow, empty store. There was a small office and a bathroom without a sink at the end of the store where it widened. No windows except for the store windows on the street and a single large window at the other end which opened onto a paved-over yard filled with Dumpsters, ancient and new.

"What kind of business are you in?" Mr. Golub asked. He was a well-dressed man of about fifty, with a shock of pepper-and-salt hair. He seemed to look per-petually apologetic about something or other.

"A gallery. Photography."

"It's perfect for that. In fact, there used to be a gallery here. In fact, about ten years ago. They had . . ." He couldn't come up with a description. He made funny little helicopter movements with his hands.

"You mean mobiles," I suggested.

"Right. That's it."

"What's the rent, Mr. Golub?"

"Three thousand a month."

"That's a bit steep," I said.

"Not for this neighborhood. It's almost SoHo."

"Actually, I only want it for a week."

"What?"

"Yes. A week."

"This isn't a hotel. We don't rent stores by the week . . . or the month . . . or the day. We offer a two-year lease."

"I can make it painless and worth your while," I an-nounced in my most savvy voice.

He found this statement of mine very funny for some reason. It also endeared me to him.

So we made a deal.

A thousand dollars for ten days.

In return for that thousand, I could do whatever I wanted in the store provided I left it exactly as I found it.

* * *

I walked into the small printing shop on Prince Street.

"Maybe you remember me?" I asked the hunched-over slip of a man whose last name, if I remembered correctly, was Ranyo.

"Should I?"

"I'm an old friend of Tony Basillio."

"I haven't seen him in years."

"He went back to the theater. He sold his chain of copy shops."

"Good for him."

"Anyway," I lied, "he says hello."

"What can I do for you?"

"Do you still have a calligrapher on staff?"

"Yes. But she isn't in today."

"I need a gallery-opening invitation. Hand-lettered. And then I need about twenty of then offset."

"Only twenty?"

"Small show," I replied.

"Write out the script," he ordered.

I did as I was told.

The invitation simply announced an exhibit by the photographer Wilma Leland Tedescu at the new gallery—Spinners—on Sullivan Street.

The date: Sunday, December 20.

The time: 3 P.M.

That was four days hence.

I pushed the script toward him. He read it and let out an exasperated groan.

"Look, lady, even if I can have this for you tomorrow night, nobody will get the invitation in time. You're talking about *this* Sunday. That's only a few days away."

"I'm not going to use the mails. They'll be hand-delivered by messengers."

"It's your call, lady. But listen . . . it's the same price if you order two hundred of them. Do you understand me?"

"I only need twenty," I said stubbornly. Actually, I needed only five.

Then I asked, "How much?"

"Three hundred dollars."

I counted out the bills without protest.

As I left he said, "To be honest with you, lady, I don't remember you at all."

"That's okay, Mr. Ranyo," I replied. "I've been told I look like a lot of people."

Everything had gone so easily . . . so fast . . . so precisely.

The invitations had been lettered, offset, picked up, and messengered anonymously over to the Dunns, the Tanners, Mickey Repp, Rita Falco, and, for good measure, Joseph Vise. I had left poor Igal out of the loop. He had had enough.

And the gallery was ready to receive the murderer.

But would the murderer show up?

Of course.

If he had removed innocuous photographs from Wilma's waiting room on the morning of the murder, he would surely do anything to prevent the world from seeing Wilma's photographs in an exhibit.

And he would have to do it the night before the opening.

This night. Or in the wee hours of the morning. Yes. It would be very late—around two or three in the morning—before the Sullivan Street pedestrian traffic vanished.

So far, so good. Except for the twinges of fear in my heart.

I was sorely tempted to call Nora or Aaron or Tony. But I didn't. As my grandmother used to say, ad nauseam, "You made your bed, you sleep in it."

I sat on a window ledge in my loft and played with my cats.

What a long, strange journey this had been.

I grew oddly at ease with my fears.

Maybe it was because I didn't have the slightest idea why the murderer was really going to raid the gallery.

I mean, I didn't know *why* he or she couldn't allow the photos to be viewed by anyone.

As for the *who*, well, it had to be one of Wilma's clients. Unless it was the mysterious Angela.

My original hunch that Wilma's murderer had been one of her clients made sense now. But that hunch seemed to have occurred a thousand years and a thousand mistakes ago.

And if this whole elaborate trap turned out to be a total failure, so what?

And if I turned out to be a demented fool playing at the fringes of reality while a double murderer skipped away . . . so what?

Was anyone else doing any better?

Aaron had long since abandoned Ann Parrish.

Rush and Morrow were still doggedly harassing Igal, fixated on him as the murderer.

And none of them had really found out anything about the life and times of Wilma Leland Tedescu except what I had given them.

Finally I began to dress. A dark green sweat suit. A short denim jacket. A knit cap.

Bushy watched me thoughtfully.

"What are you looking at?" I demanded. He gave me one of his wise yawns.

"So you think I need a weapon, do you?"

I went into the kitchen and selected a short, ugly knife with one serrated edge.

Then I threw a roll of tape into my bag with the contact-sheet strips, a small tape recorder that Tony had given me two years ago, with the requisite batteries. "To dictate notes for your autobiography," he had said.

"If anything happens to me, cats, don't mourn. Felix and Alison will take care of you. You'll have nothing but thick bouillabaisse the rest of your natural lives."

I left the loft and walked slowly through the dark streets filled with people about to become Saturday night revelers.

When I got to my new gallery I stared at it happily. Even in the dim light of a streetlamp it presented itself as a jewel of authenticity.

Not quite chic. Not quite funky.

I had paid a neighborhood kid to spray paint SPIN-NERS on the front window, graffiti style.

And I had pasted one of the invitations inside the front door so that people passing could read it through the door pane. It just seemed the proper thing to do.

I walked in, closed the door behind me, and switched on the light.

There was no time for musing.

First I taped the contact strips to the wall.

Then I figured out how the murderer would enter. It would probably be through the back window. Push it up from the outside, or break it; remove the photos, climb out. Simple.

To facilitate the intruder's access, I opened the back window of the store. Not much. About an inch.

Next I had to figure out where I would wait for the intruder . . . in what quadrant of my sticky web.

Since he or she was probably coming in through the back window, I situated myself in the small bend where the store widened to accommodate the office and the bathroom. This way the intruder would walk right past me, providing I was down low, and proceed into the display space.

I switched the light off, sat down on the floor, made myself comfortable, and began my vigil.

Oh, what a vigil it was to be. I saw myself as Alice Nestleton, ex-actress, ex-cat-sitter, and now Spider extraordinaire.

For a brief moment I even had the fantasy that my limbs were covered with a delicate downy glue.

I took the small tape recorder out of my bag and placed it on the floor next to me.

It was soothing just sitting there in the gloom of the gallery. My back was cushioned by the wall . . . my legs stretched out. It was a bit chilly, but not too bad.

The knife! Where was the knife? I searched the bag. It was there. I took it out, unwrapped it, and placed it, a bit dramatically, on the far side of the recorder.

I closed my eyes. Yes, oddly soothing.

An hour passed. I grew bored. I pressed the button on the recording machine and started a ridiculous monologue for posterity.

"Hello," I said in a loud, hoarse whisper. "This is Alice Nestleton of ABC News. It is past midnight. I am here on a dangerous stakeout for the NYPD. The quarry is a double murderer who, until now, has escaped all efforts to apprehend him. The lure is a series of brilliant photographic images that he must have to ease his psychotic mind. Yes, this is the front line. . . ."

Then I felt ridiculous and shut the damn thing off. I

was hungry. Anxiety either makes you hungry or takes away your appetite completely. I began thinking about the cream pie in the freezer at home.

I heard laughing outside.

I shivered a bit, grabbed my knife, and leaned forward. I could see dimly through the store window. A group of young men and women singing and staggering. One was peering through the front window and yelling something lewd.

Then one of his alcohol-soaked cohorts called to him and they all moved off loudly.

But they had profoundly activated my fear.

Suddenly I realized what a fool I had been in acting alone. What was I doing there all alone waiting for a killer who most likely had in his pocket the same gun he had used to assassinate Wilma Tedescu and Ann Parrish? Would he tie a little apron around *my* corpse also?

I wanted to get up and run—through the door and out onto the street and all the way back to my loft and my cats.

The sweat was like cold jewels along the top of my forehead. My stomach was flipping over and over.

Calm down. Calm down. Calm down, I kept reciting to myself in singsong.

I flipped the cassette player back on. Anything to get my head straight and relax.

I started to recite lines from Euripides' *Trojan*

Women. Lines I knew as well as I knew my telephone number. O ye gods! What treacherous friends you are!

"But where fate's misery plunged one into black despair—whom else can one summon but the gods.

"Let me then—"

A sudden whoosh of sound—outside my performance.

I quickly shut off the machine. My toes were going numb. I cocked my head.

Again it came. It sounded like wind.

Oh my God! Was he coming through that back window now? My mouth felt baked. I closed my eyes.

Open them, you silly woman, I said to myself. I looked toward the rear window reluctantly. No. Nothing. Maybe it had been a family of Beatrix Potter mice setting out on a picnic.

My whole body relaxed. I switched the machine on and started to continue my Hecabe performance, a role I must have played eleven times.

But the next line escaped me. This was crazy. Alice Nestleton never forgets her lines.

Okay. Go to the next remembered line . . . go to the middle of the lament.

"My virgin daughters, whom I had nurtured to be exquisite gifts to heroes, are stolen from me.

"Taken by base enemies. Doomed never to see their mother again.

"And now comes the final agony. . . ."

I heard glass breaking. It was the front door.

My body went rigid. A hand was pushing through the shattered panel to grasp the inside knob. I pressed my body back against the wall. I started to breathe heavily.

The door opened and closed. Someone was inside. The figure moved slowly.

A small flashlight beam scanned the walls.

It was a woman. Could it be the daughter? Could it finally be that Angela?

The beam was looking for the exhibit. It found only those pathetic strips of contact sheets.

Then the figure started to pull the taped strips from the wall.

Now! I steeled myself. Now or never!

I slid up against the wall, picking up the knife as I moved.

And then I raced down the narrow store to the wall light switch and flicked it on.

The figure yelled something incoherent.

We were facing each other in the light. It wasn't any kind of Angela.

It was Leslie Tanner, the jewelry designer, in a baggy black outfit, her hair tied back.

I couldn't catch my breath. I couldn't talk. I kept the knife pointed at her as if I knew what to do with it.

She was five feet away, the contact strips still in her hand.

She looked at me wildly, then turned her head toward the door. She was going to bolt. I knew it.

My voice came back.

"It won't work. There are two plainclothes detectives in an unmarked car across the street, watching us."

"You're lying," she said. She was right, but she hesitated.

"Do you think I'd be that stupid—to come here alone?"

She pondered. She didn't move.

"Why did you break in here? What are those images about?"

She stared at me blankly. She didn't respond.

"Why did you kill Wilma?"

She closed her eyes and swayed.

"It's too late for silence," I shouted.

Then I lied again, intuitively, almost desperately.

"Don't you understand? At this very moment a search warrant is being executed in your apartment. Your husband has probably already been placed under arrest."

"You people know nothing." She had opened her eyes defiantly.

"How wrong you are. There were other contact strips that the police have now. That I didn't use as bait. And those are very interesting. They're nude self-portraits by a murdered woman that point to her killer. She is naked except for some jewelry around her neck. Your jewelry. It was Wilma's insurance policy that her killer would be caught."

I hadn't planned that lie, hadn't prepared an

elaborate set of falsehoods to persuade the murderer to talk. I was just winging it. Luckily, it worked.

Leslie Tanner crumbled like a saltine.

"Yes. It was Wyatt who killed her. But you don't understand. He had to. There was no other way out."

"What do you mean, 'no way out'?"

"Wilma wouldn't let us quit."

"Quit what?"

She shook the strips in her hand.

"It was an ugly thing. When Wyatt and I appraised jewelry in estates, we looked for vulnerable widows. Then we stole photos of the dead husbands and gave them to Wilma. She made fake collages that showed her and the husband in what could be called a compromising situation. Then she took them to the widow. Wilma threatened to show the photos to the woman's family or to contest the will on the grounds that she had been the husband's secret common-law wife for many years. Unless she was paid off immediately.

"Sometimes it didn't work. Sometimes it did. There were women who would pay anything not to let their children see such photos of their father. And there were women who needed a quick resolution of the estate and could not afford a court battle. These kinds of women would even borrow fifty or sixty thousand dollars against the estate to pay Wilma off."

Leslie Tanner shook her head. As if the whole ugly thing were too much to bear, upon recollection. But she couldn't stop now. The confession had been cathartic.

"But Wyatt and I wanted out. We no longer even needed the money. Wilma wouldn't let us quit. She threatened to go to the police and turn us all in. She said we'd all go down together if Wyatt and I tried to pull out. And we knew she would do it. She bragged to us how she would do anything for Angela. She bragged how she had murdered Ann Parrish."

"Wait. What are you talking about? Wilma murdered Ann Parrish?" I couldn't believe what I was hearing.

"Yes."

"But why?"

"As I said, for Angela."

"Angela? Why kill for Angela?"

"She was a disturbed child. Wilma took her to a psychiatrist named James Parrish who was using a new treatment for early-onset schizophrenia. It included massive doses of vitamin C and B_{12}. Wilma was nervous about what was then a new treatment. Parrish told her it was safe and natural—as natural as chicken soup made in the kitchen. Wilma agreed. For whatever reason, it didn't work. Angela became hopelessly psychotic and had to be placed in a state mental hospital. The child was abused there. Wilma put her into a private hospital.

"It cost her thousands of dollars a month. She needed money all the time. She blamed the psychiatrist for her daughter's mental breakdown and her financial struggle. She grew to hate him. But he died before she could seek vengeance. So she threatened, hunted down, and murdered his petrified wife."

"Is Angela still alive?"

"Yes. And still hospitalized."

"The apron, Leslie. Tell me about the apron."

She started to sob. Her words came out in gasps.

"Wilma told us the story a dozen times . . . with relish . . . to frighten us. How she made the widow put on a small kitchen apron before she killed her. Because her dead husband had claimed his treatment was as safe as chicken soup made in the kitchen."

"Why did your husband copycat the murder?"

"Because he had begun to hate Wilma Tedescu as much as Wilma hated Parrish and his wife. It became a psychodrama for poor Wyatt. He wanted to kill the witch the exact same way she had killed. It was the only method he had to purge himself of her hold on him . . . and me."

How sad that was. It revolted me. I felt weak. I slid down along the wall until I was in a sitting position. It was hard for me to fathom Wilma Leland Tedescu. She was a caring mother. She was a woman with a rare gift for healing felines. And yet, she was a brutal, vindictive killer and extortionist.

I looked up. Leslie Tanner hadn't moved. She had a strange look on her face, like she was seeking help from me.

I turned away. My eyes caught a flicker of red light near my bag at the other end of the store.

I had forgotten to turn the little tape recorder off when the door glass was shattered. I smiled. A good actress needs luck as well as talent.

Chapter 15

It was a lovely evening in my loft. Moonlight rafting through the windows. The winter solstice past; Christmas almost here. All that was missing was a cozy fireplace. I'd have to talk to Felix, my Santa Claus of a landlord, about putting one in.

Nora and I sat at the small dining table. Bushy was asleep on a window ledge. Pancho was waiting to pounce on—or run from—an enemy that was about to emerge from the walk-in closet. I assumed that in Pancho's mind this enemy was a seven-foot killer mouse with a deadly ray gun.

Nora was opening one of the two bottles of champagne she had brought, along with a take-out platter from none other than Petrossian, the caviar restaurant.

"You were brilliant, Alice. Absolutely brilliant."

"Thank you."

"And the most brilliant thing," Nora continued, "was that little lie off the top of your head that broke the dam."

"You mean when I said that there existed photos of a naked Wilma wearing jewelry made by the Tanners?"

"Yes. How did you ever think of that?"

"It just popped out. Like when you're onstage and another actor forgets his lines. The only way to help him, there and then, is to ad-lib any kind of nonsense until he gets back on track."

The doorbell rang just then. Three short, insistent blasts. I left the table and buzzed back.

"Expecting company?" Nora asked.

"No."

"Fess up, Alice. It's the UPS guy, isn't it? You've been ordering clothes from catalogues, haven't you? Let me warn you. It's a very dangerous addiction. But some of the UPS fellas are mighty cute."

I laughed. "Honest, I haven't ordered anything. The only thing I'm expecting is some yarn. I decided to knit you a pot holder for Christmas, which, according to my calculations, should be ready for you around Easter."

"What I always needed," Nora replied happily.

"I'll bet it's something from my agent," I said.

I turned back toward the steps and waited. I heard the delivery man climbing, very slowly.

Then he reached my landing.

My God! It was Tony Basillio. He was wearing false whiskers, snowy white.

He stood in front of me holding a package and grinning.

"Tony! What are you doing here?" I asked, starting to giggle in spite of the intrusion.

All he said was, "Ho, ho, ho."

And then I saw he was wearing a Santa hat. A really oversized one with a huge pom-pom.

"You're a few days early, aren't you, Mr. Kringle?"

"What an unchristian greeting," he replied, and walked past me into the loft.

I followed him and closed the door. Tony gave a cheery hello to Nora. Her greeting to him was decidedly cool. I remembered that the last time they had met was under stressful circumstances. During the breakup, Tony had stormed into Nora's bistro, where I was seated in a booth with Aaron Stoner. And Tony had been verbally abusive to everyone.

"Actually, the elves and I are ahead of schedule this year. And I don't have to point out to you that you have no chimney. So . . . here I am."

He placed his package on the table.

"At least you haven't come empty-handed," I said.

"In fact," he said, "this gift is not from me."

"It isn't? Who is it from?"

"A Rumanian gentleman by the name of Tedescu."

"What!"

"That's right. I got a telephone call from this crazy

Rumanian. Igal. He had called Rita Falco and said he had something for you but didn't feel right about delivering it himself. He wanted to know how to get it to you, so Rita gave him my number, knowing that we were friends."

"Are we friends, Tony?" I interjected.

Bushy, meanwhile, who had a very troubled friendship with Tony, ambled over and rubbed against his legs. Tony teased him a lot, but Bushy nonetheless knew Tony as a mark who was always good for a few tidbits on the sly at suppertime.

Tony brushed off my question. "There's more to the story, by the way. Want to hear it?" he asked.

Nora shrugged.

"Sure," I said. "Let's hear it."

"Okay. He says to me that he also wants to show Alice Nestleton that he is on his way to becoming a good American . . . that he has resolved to love Santa Claus in—how did he put it?—yes . . . he said in all his manifestations. So, could I, me, Tony, wear a Santa Claus hat when I delivered it."

I looked at Nora. She looked at me.

"Does this sound credible?" I asked her.

"Hardly."

"Could I make up a story like this?" Tony raised his hands in mock despair.

Then he caught sight of Pancho along the far wall. Panch was crouched low and glaring at the intruder. This was even worse than his paranoid delusions; this was a real threat: a bewhiskered killer mouse dressed in red. Poor Pancho started a wild dash to safety.

Then Tony spotted the food and drink on the table.

"What's this? Caviar? And champagne! My lucky day. I am famished." He gave me an imploring look.

"Ask Nora," I said. "She paid for it."

"Help yourself," Nora said. "I know how much you like *delicacies*."

Tony, who was already at the caviar, stopped. He had picked up on the venom in Nora's use of the word "delicacies."

"What's that supposed to mean, Nora?" he asked, his voice growing thick and dark.

"Oh, come off it, Tony. Everyone knows you like certain kinds of delicacies."

"Is that right?" Tony removed the fake white beard and thrust out his chin.

"Yes, that is right," Nora countered, just as combative. "So why be so defensive about it?"

"Name some of these delicacies."

"Are you sure you want me to?"

"Yes."

"Well," Nora said, adopting her innocent tone, "everyone knows that you have this thing for young actresses. And for a man your age, they certainly are delicacies."

Basillio stood there, twirling an empty champagne flute in his hands. He gave me a filthy look, as if I had betrayed a monumental confidence.

He finally said to Nora: "The Swede here, the lady you know as Alice Nestleton, has a very rich fantasy life."

"Don't we all?" Nora retorted.

"Stop this, both of you!" I spoke at last. "No more of this. We're having a party here, not a prizefight."

Each looked my way, half abashed, half defiant.

"You heard what I said, children," I cautioned. "Let's get back to our little party. Come on, let's open the gift."

My orders were heeded. After all, it was my loft. We all circled the table.

I opened the package carefully, faking a bit more girlish enthusiasm than I was genuinely feeling.

There was a card.

On the upper right hand of the card was a lovely little watercolor of a snoozing feline with three mice playing hopscotch around her tail.

The writing on the card said simply, "Thank you, Alice Nestleton. With respect, Igal."

I turned the box over.

Out rolled six brightly colored spinning tops.

Nora whooped, grabbed one, and set it turning on the table. It spun right off and onto the floor.

Soon Tony and I joined in and we had the whole loft awhirl with the objects.

Then I stilled mine with the flat of my hand. Nora and Tony followed suit.

"I just had an inspiration," I declared.

My guests waited expectantly.

"Do you know what I give Pancho every year for Christmas?"

"If I remember right, saffron rice," Tony said.

"That's right. Every year I cater to his very strange whim. Do you know any other cats who'd kill for saffron rice? I never met any. But listen. This year I'm not going to give him the rice. I'm going to give him a gift that's a thousand times more valuable. I'm going to give Pancho his sanity back."

Then I called out: "Pancho! Get ready for your therapy session."

I turned back to Nora. "And after I cure Pancho, do you know what I'm going to do?"

"Have more champagne," Nora said. And, indeed, she filled all our glasses.

"Besides that," I said. "After I fix Pancho up with these tops the way Wilma would have . . . I'm going to pack them into a little black bag and make some house calls."

"To who?"

"What about to disaffected males?"

"Excellent." We both enjoyed watching Tony squirm.

"As long as you don't pack any dumb little aprons," Nora said.

"No aprons at all," I agreed.

We started to concentrate on the caviar and the crackers and champagne. I turned on the Newark jazz station at the bottom of the FM dial and we listened to

John Coltrane. The loft grew friendly and warm. Tony and Nora made up with a friendly kiss. I could see the Christmas lights that had been strung along the top floor of the warehouse across the street. Red and blue and green and some colors I couldn't even identify.

"You're looking at those lights, aren't you?" Tony asked.

"I never noticed them before."

"Do you remember the loft party where the lights were inside? The same kind of lights, tacked up around the ceiling."

"No, I don't."

Tony said to Nora, "Your friend has a very bad memory."

"Bad memory, good heart," Nora said indulgently.

Tony turned back to me. "Well, I'll refresh your memory. It was about 1974 or so. It was in Billy Luxor's loft, on West Twenty-third. We bumped into each other again. We hadn't seen each other since acting school . . . since the Dramatic Workshop."

Billy Luxor. Billy Luxor. I repeated the name a couple of times. It was vaguely familiar.

"He was short and well built and very handsome. Blond. He acted in a couple of Quintero productions. I think he teaches at U Cal Riverside now."

"I remember him, Tony, but not the party."

"Everyone was broke then. No caviar and champagne. We had specials and baked beans and long-necked bottles of the worst beer I ever tasted. But he had a Christmas tree. And instead of ornaments there were cardboard cutouts of various English actors in all kinds of lewd positions."

Nora laughed. "Those were the days when everyone hated the poor English actors."

"With good reason," Tony said. "They had kidnapped Broadway. You couldn't get a role unless you spoke high British or low Cockney. Anyway, it was a wonderful party." He lost himself in reverie for a moment and then said, "I remember what you were wearing, Swede."

"What?"

"A pair of beat-up jeans and a thick green sweater with ragged sleeves. And you had one of those short Jean Seberg cuts. You were beautiful."

After a few moments of silence Nora began to shift around on the sofa, obviously uncomfortable. "I have to get back to the bistro," she said, starting to search for her coat.

"No, don't go, Nora, please don't go. It's your party as well as mine."

She gave me a long, wistful look and shook her head. "I have to get back," she said. She was lying and she knew I knew it. I tried to tell her that there was nothing between Tony and me anymore . . . that I considered her friendship more important than his reminiscences . . . but all that came out of my mouth were clichés about what a crime it is to leave before a good bottle of champagne is all gone.

The minute I closed the door behind her, I turned to Tony and said, "It was nice of you to bring that package, Tony." And I kept my hand on the doorknob, signaling that it was now time for him to leave also.

But he refused to recognize the cue. He took off his big Santa hat and fiddled with it.

"What are you doing Christmas Eve?" he asked.

"Staying home."

"What are you doing Christmas Day?"

"Having dinner with my niece."

"What about New Year's Eve?"

"Staying home, probably."

"It wasn't a good year for you, was it, Swede?"

"I've seen better."

"You've seen a lot better. Maybe the new year will turn up aces."

"A nice thought, Tony. Optimistic but nice."

"What kind of year would you like?"

I dropped my hand from the doorknob but didn't move away from the door.

"I think," I said, "I'd like a year where I see no violence, where I get two good parts, where Pancho learns how to enjoy life, where I don't have to—"

I stopped suddenly. Tony had turned away as if he could no longer listen to me. He looked as if he had suddenly become ill.

I took two steps toward him.

He turned back to me. There were tears in his eyes.

"Tony, are you okay? Listen, Tony, I—"

He held up his hands to show that he was okay. "I just want you to forgive me, Swede," he said. "I want you to forgive me for every bad thing I did."

Then my own tears began to fall.

The next moment we were holding each other, tightly, very tightly.

He was saying something, but I couldn't hear, or didn't want to hear.

"What did you just say, Tony?" I asked. "Was it something about the night?"

"Yes," he said softly, brushing away the last of my tears. "To all, a good night."